CROSSWORDS

W
CROSS
R
D
S

A NOVEL

BY

[signature: F. Jack Frerker]

JACK FRERKER

PAX PUBLICATIONS — OLYMPIA, WASHINGTON

Published by PAX Publications, 1405 Eastview Court NW, Olympia WA 98502

Printed in the U S A, by Bang Printing of Brainerd MN

This is a work of fiction. All names, characters and incidents are from the author's imagination or used fictitiously. Reference to real persons is not intended and should not be inferred.

LIBRARY OF CONGRESS CATALOGING-IN-PUBLICATION DATA

Frerker, Jack, 1937 –
    CROSSWORDS
    ISBN 978-0-9740080-7-3

OTHER NOVELS BY JACK FRERKER
    HEAT
    SOLSTICE
    CONNECTIONS
    CONSPIRACY
    MONKSBANE
    RECOLLECTIONS

ACKNOWLEDGMENTS

Thanks to the good Lord for another year of life, ministry and literary endeavors. Life continues to surprise, enlighten and encourage me. Who says that retirement times are not the golden years?

And thanks again to my trusted team, without whom my books would not see the light of day: Richard Swanson, whose electronic genius makes my website beautiful and the text of my books line up professionally; and Paula Buckner, Tom Vickery and Joe Weir, whose friendships have lasted despite their having to pick a path through my sometimes weird approach to the English language in order to make sense of it via their proofreading and editing abilities; and to Scott Whitney and Erica Sotak of Whitney Design, who have become the newest members of the team by providing the cover to this book.

And, finally: my gratitude to all of you who have humored me by reading these literary efforts of mine over the years. You are intrepid souls.

Jack Frerker

FOR THOSE WHO HELP SOLVE

THE PUZZLES OF LIFE FOR OTHERS

CHAPTER 1

It was neither the best of times nor the worst, just another typical day in the ministerial life of Father John Wintermann, though not such a bad one, at that, for early September. The weather was no longer steamy, the light was beginning to take on the crisp, slanted autumnal look of his favorite season of year, though the leaves hadn't turned yet, let alone begun to fall from the trees, and the only thing on his mind as he drove out onto the streets of Algoma was the satisfying prospect of a delightful visit with Fred and Frieda at their pharmacy while searching out a bottle of mouthwash. The gossip, he hoped, would be added entertainment and enough to sustain him the rest of the day. There might even be an ice cream concoction to sweeten the moment.

He had already told the Beckers about his time in the Northwest at the Abbey of Saint Martin. Today would bring their opportunity to fill him in on the latest for Algoma and environs. They were not to disappoint.

"Been a spate of vandalisms around town. Kids, probably, stealing newspapers out of roadside boxes. Ain't no pile of 'em been found, so the question is what they're doin' with 'em." Father John nodded sagaciously at that tidbit, grateful that his paper had so far remained untouched.

"The Farrells are back from Florida. Don't know why they'd want to go there in the hot months and come back here for winter. They're no spring chickens any more, either, so they ain't comin' back for winter sports." Frieda smiled at her own whimsy.

Fred took over. "Doc Littleton's handwriting is gettin' worse and worse. Had to call him the other day to be sure I was readin' his latest scrips right. I even suggested his office girl type them up so's he could just sign 'em. Must have thought I was joking because he laughed. It wasn't no joke!" Frieda and Father John laughed, however, and Fred acknowledged that maybe there was some humor in it.

His old friends rang the changes on all the town trivia they could think of, and Father John left a half-hour later thoroughly caught up on most everything that makes living in Algoma endurable, even fun. He had reluctantly turned down an ice cream something-or-other from Frieda, citing fear of his personal physician, whom he would be seeing later that week. "No sense giving Doctor Wilson the satisfaction of belittling me again for little or no weight loss," he told them. "I am actually down a pound and I might even make 2 pounds by my visit, especially if I stay away from ice cream a few more days." Fred and Frieda weren't sure if that was a little joke. Both decided to nod conspiratorially, just in case. They knew they had made the right decision when Father John didn't look disappointed at their response.

When he left the always-cool confines of the fountain/pharmacy, the priest drove leisurely through town on the off chance of seeing something in need of his pastoral attention or at very least his snooping into. Finding nothing after fifteen minutes, he decided to waste no more gas or time and headed home. When he retrieved his newspaper, he remembered what his friends had reported. His box remained unraided, though, as he pulled the Post-

Dispatch out of its slot, something fell to the ground. He was amused to see that it looked like a crossword puzzle. On an otherwise blank set of little black and white squares was the single word *INTRIGUED*, each letter neatly penciled in small, block printing. Nothing gave a clue as to its origin or what it should portend. He stuffed it into the folds of the newspaper and carried the entire bundle inside to peruse with his noontime sandwich and coffee.

Hunger pangs set in an hour later, and he was about to grill a ham and cheese sandwich when the phone rang. That conversation finished, he got back to making his lunch and remembered a fresh tomato in the refrigerator. He retrieved it, poured a cup of coffee and finally sat down with his newspaper to a late repast around one o'clock. He saw the small piece of paper poking out from the sports page and pushed it aside for later. There it sat forgotten, however, for the next several days and would have been swept into the trash by Maisie on Saturday, had he not received another such item on Friday morning. Once again it was with his newspaper, and once again nothing was on the small piece of paper except three words in their little crossword squares: *YOU SHOULD BE*.

Now he was hooked. "What the devil can this mean?" he said aloud. Similar ruminations were to trouble him the rest of that day until he finally decided that someone was teasing him into trying to figure out the what and why of the two notes. With that, he was able to shove the distractions from his mind and not revisit them for over a week. Meantime, he could now attend to important things, like touching up his homily and visiting two parishioners in the hospital.

Life comfortably returned to the routines of parish life after his retreat in the Northwest, and as autumn began to be felt, he silently thanked God for the peace of mind garnered from his week with the Benedictines in Washington. He made a mental note to say as much by phone to the abbot of Saint Martin's Abbey after his weekend Masses.

CHAPTER 2

His homily that weekend was better than average, if he had to say so himself, although it boosted his confidence when several parishioners had favorable critiques to share with him. Later Sunday afternoon, he remembered the two cryptic notes and briefly tried to untangle the mystery of where they had come from and why. But football on television soon banished them from his mind, and he didn't resume pondering over them again until the following morning when he got his paper and discovered a third note tucked inside. This one was more pointed: *YOU ARE IT*. Now Father John was sure there was some kind of game afoot and wasn't sure how friendly it was going to turn out to be.

Then he remembered having seen something in the St. Louis Post-Dispatch about some new kind of crossword game. He wasn't sure when he had seen it and couldn't remember many details about it. It took some minutes to realize that he could probably find it on the paper's website.

Not much at home in the world of computers, it took him half an hour to find what he was looking for. He got to the site readily enough, but delving his way through it was frustratingly slow. When he finally found what he was looking for, he felt his efforts rewarded. A loyal reader had met the crossword editor at a party and suggested a new kind of puzzle, one involving crimes that were to be solved piece-meal in crossword fashion: each clue somehow connecting to a previous clue in a cleverly constructed crossword puzzle.

The editor liked the idea and contacted the man for further brainstorming. Armed with the results of their discussion, the editor put the idea to a handful of his puzzle contributors, and several months later one of them provided just such a puzzle to the Post. The article that Father John had found went into great detail about the complex construction of such a puzzle, and the submitted entry was run in that same edition of the paper. It had modest success, and the originator of the idea eventually submitted a second puzzle that made its way into the paper. Soon, a puzzle like that had begun to appear in the Post every few weeks.

And there the matter would have no doubt ended, had not St. Louis police reported a murder several weeks after the appearance of the third puzzle with similarities to the puzzle scenario. The Post's editor and the police were disturbed. There was nothing in the paper's archives about a solution to that real-life murder, but Father John didn't like the eerie similarities to the notes in his paper box. This would definitely bear watching.

It then occurred to him to see if the words he received might fit into some sort of larger puzzle, but he got nowhere with the combinations and finally put the three notes along with his doodlings aside. But this time he didn't forget about them. He knew exactly where they were, and he planned to retrieve them the moment something else surfaced … if, indeed, it ever did.

CHAPTER 3

By Tuesday morning, Father John had successfully put all pesky puzzle thoughts out of his mind and was able to celebrate Mass prayerfully. Afterward, he remembered that his friend, Father Louis in Okawville, had invited him to attend the wheat festival there and promised to treat him to a meal of festival food. But that had been a number of weeks earlier and he was no longer sure on which September weekend the annual festival was celebrated. He had never been to that particular celebration, although he'd attended many such others in Southern Illinois, from the Murphysboro Apple and the Cobden Peach festivals to the numerous street fairs almost every little town has each summer. And, of course, attendance at the yearly church picnics around the diocese was mandatory; the only thing keeping him away from those being an occasional summer cold or a parishioner's wake.

He made a mental note to drive into the country after lunch to see the Pattersons and check on Lori's pregnancy. It was also a good excuse to check out crops on the nearby farms while he was getting a lead on when that young couple might want to schedule their child's baptism. He liked to pencil in such things, as it gave him the flexibility of liturgically blending in other family celebrations, such as wedding anniversaries and birthdays. Such things were prime candidates for making Sunday Mass more a community affair.

Lunch finished and just before he planned to leave for the country, he received a call from an elderly parishioner. The gentleman was rather agitated and wanted to talk about all the reports he was hearing about *pedalphelia*. Father John could hardly keep from laughing at the man's inept pronunciation but promised to stop at his home on his way out of town. Having decided to combine the two outings, he got into his aging Taurus and headed south out of town.

He stopped first at the old man's place on Algoma's outskirts, hoping he could get things clarified as to terminology without caving in to any laughter. That conversation actually went better than expected. He was able to calm the man's concerns by telling him that the diocese was on top of that awful outbreak, and there had been no cases here for a number of years. What the man had recently been hearing about, bad as it was, had come from dioceses elsewhere in the country. Yes, he told him, we did have some of that happen here, but it looked now like that was all behind us. That seemed to relieve the old gentleman. Father John thought it best not to mention the large settlement from one of those earlier cases that was pending in court. If that came to light and further agitated the old man, he'd deal with it at that time. The correct pronunciation of the word in question never came up.

He headed into the countryside, where he saw fields of soybeans already turned yellow and corn that was morphing into tannish brown despite the previous week's rains that promised bright-leaved autumn scenery in the coming weeks.

The Pattersons were a bubbly and delightful young farm couple, and he was happy to spend an hour or more with them. Both were very excited about the impending birth of their firstborn. No, they said, they didn't know its gender yet and wanted to be surprised. And yes, they also had names picked out, saints' names at that, so Father John was not able to make his usual joke about naming the baby Paphnutius, in honor of an actual early Roman martyr. Given the probable due date the doctor had given them, the baptism could tentatively be celebrated the third weekend in October, and Father John promised to pencil that in when he returned to the rectory. On his way out the door, they presented him with a jar of homemade strawberry jam, which he readily confessed would not last long on his breakfast table. He silently breathed a sigh of gratitude that his recent visit to the doctor had confirmed a 2-pound weight loss, and for at least the near future, some jelly on his breakfast toast shouldn't occasion any troubling guilt trips.

On his way back into town, the jam on the seat beside him was a reminder that fresh bread would be nice, so he stopped at Henry Lohman's store for a loaf of either multigrain or whole wheat and perhaps some breakfast sausages. There might also be some local gossip if Hy proved not too busy. He also knew full well that the proprietor might try to sell him another package of meat, depending on what was on sale.

He was in luck. No one was at the meat counter, and he had Hy all to himself. The only sale item that week was extra-lean ground beef, so Father John contented himself with the sausages and a generous serving of Hy's spin on news around the county. On his way to the front of the store some minutes later, he grabbed a hefty loaf of multigrain bread, harrumphing quietly about its price. He had learned nothing earth-shattering from his butcher friend, but the minutes at the meat counter were golden nonetheless. He liked Hy and regretted not spending more time over the past few months tending to their friendship.

Fall was his favorite season, and that year it had already begun to settle in ever so slowly well before it's official moment in late September. The leaves had not yet begun to turn but the slanting light gave a distinctive crisp look to things in the early part of the day before turning faint in late afternoon. The smell of burning leaves was also already occasionally in the air, something Father John particularly liked about autumn.

His love affair with that odor had begun eons before, when he went off to the high school seminary. He hadn't particularly relished raking leaves at home during grade school, but ironically it was that smell that somehow grabbed him at the Belleville seminary and made him strangely nostalgic. Students there were allowed, in fact required, to rake the many leaves on the school's campus, and he joined his cohorts only to discover that he now enjoyed the chore. He never understood that metamorphosis, but it left him with an even greater attachment to the season, and thereafter, whenever he smelled burning leaves, he was reminded of high school seminary and the quirkiness of life.

That distinctive autumn smell greeted him once he came outside Hy's establishment, so he decided to drive through town with his windows down in quest of burning leaves. He found some several blocks away where the homeowner was still busy raking, and though he didn't know the man, he decided to stop for a chat.

Good Methodist that the older fellow turned out to be, he had a lovely chat with Father John, nonetheless, spending a quarter of an hour mostly in discussion about the city council's decision to assess a special tax to increase funding for the city park and swimming pool. Both men agreed that the move was long overdue and that city youth would be the better for it. The pool was already closed until next year's Memorial Day weekend, so the tax wouldn't be levied until the next spring. The relatively few critics in town would have ample time to lick their wounds and set aside the modest amount the tax would impose. Both men expected little further outcry about that council decision.

When he finally returned to the rectory, he found a message on the answering machine. A lady wanted to talk. Father John knew her and assumed it was another complaint about the bullying of her son, Randy, who had always been small and presented a tempting target to bigger boys. The taunting had begun even before Randy entered grade school. His buddies began calling him *Bandy*, the nickname for a bantam rooster and therefore a convenient way to make fun of his size. Lost on them was the fact that the nickname also targeted the rooster in question as a ferocious fighter.

Numerous times after the boy entered Saint Helena's school, principal and teachers had been badgered by the worried mother into doing something about her son's treatment at the hands of other boys. Again and again they would pull the offending children aside with warnings that worked for a week or two, but the problem had always reasserted itself. Father John, for his part, had long ago found himself praying earnestly for Randy to hit a growth spurt.

He phoned her and she came over right away. When they sat down to talk, however, it wasn't about the boy. What Father John heard was an almost stereotypic drunken spouse story of physical abuse, something that was very much news to Father John. So far as he could remember, nothing like that had ever happened in his time in Algoma, let alone at Saint Helena's parish.

She talked for a long time, and he listened with genuine and growing concern. It had gone on for a number of years, starting just before the birth of their only child. She wasn't sure if that meant the man hadn't really wanted children or was indicative of something else. He also wondered how much that had affected their son.

Father John probed as to whether it was possibly a product of the man's family history. With no clear indications about that, he gently asked about the man's work history. He learned that he hadn't been happy for some time with how he was treated there, and he noted that the woman's extreme sadness over her husband's disappointment and resentment had started late in her pregnancy.

John Henry Wintermann had always been perched well beneath chancery radar. Not only was he the kind of pedestrian parish priest who wouldn't set off warning sirens, he didn't even remotely harbor most of the edgy thoughts that often call upstarts to the attention of zealous clerical bureaucrats as they scan the horizon for heresies and new-fangled theologies. Whatever in his common-sense

12

pastoral approach to his people's pain might be considered off-center from the party line was largely confined to confessional moments and never wandered into the light via sermons or public pronouncements. In fact, it never occurred to him that the bishop might find such confessional advice or pastoral practice questionable. How could he? They were too reasonable and as such just what his people needed for them to find a spiritual way out of any difficulty life sent their way.

So it was that in this current people-patching moment with Mrs. Mandeville he dared to suggest the possibility of her leaving her husband. He began gently probing: "Where did you hail from, Genevieve? I know you weren't born here."

"I'm originally from Pennsylvania, Father."

"And your husband?"

"From Connecticut."

"So, how'd you meet, then?"

"He was an airman at Scott Field. I was doing a degree in education at St. Louis University, and we met at a school mixer. A number of airmen would come across the river and, as it turned out, a number of them met future wives at dances like that. But why are you curious about that?"

"I was just wondering if there was a place to go with Randy … to get away from the abuse, at least a while … and be safe from your husband coming after you."

She studied him for what seemed a long time. "I had thought about that. I'm surprised to hear it here. Doesn't the church frown on that?"

"Not in circumstances like these, no, Genevieve. At least, not necessarily."

Numerous clerics — at least party-line folks — might agree with her assessment: protect marriage at any cost! But that sounded utterly foolish to Father Wintermann in cases like this. Emboldened by the privileged nature of this conversation — enjoying as it did the same sacred secrecy as confession — he not only introduced the idea, but pressed it. "You needn't take that from anyone, not even, and perhaps especially, your husband. However, we should talk this out: maybe there are other options that might encourage your husband to change his ways."

The better part of an hour later, a calmer Genevieve Mandeville had determined to contact her parents and begin the process of leaving her husband, however temporarily or permanently that might turn out to be. Father John promised to be available should she need further counsel. And, by all means, his prayers would be hers as well.

CHAPTER 4

The next morning Father John awoke, as he had for the past several years, to the morning news on the St. Louis NPR station. Hearing a report from Africa by Ofeibea Quist-Arcton, he remembered Father Olav at the Abbey in Washington. He had complained about the strange names on NPR. While he was chuckling about that conversation from last summer, he heard another report, this one by Neda Ulaby. Olav had been right: there *are* very different sounding names on Public Radio. In fact, these two female correspondents had strange first *and* last names. He figured that Quist-Arcton was British but couldn't puzzle out the ethnic background for "Ulaby." He guessed it might be Mideastern.

There was also Dina Temple-Raston, another hyphenated name. She *sounded* very American, but he wasn't sure that was in fact the case. This whole business of such strange names on the national airwaves was altogether curious. Such was certainly not the case in Algoma, though the phenomenon was not totally unknown in town. Googie Gilden knew enough about it to have run at the mouth to Father John some weeks earlier.

"Like me, they're Jewish, don't you know."

"Not all of them, Googie."

"A lot of them are, like Scott Simon."

"He's half Jewish. His mother's Catholic, I'm pretty sure. But he doesn't have one of those strange names … like your own, for goodness sakes, Googie," he said emphasizing the man's nickname.

Googie was one of only two tailors in Algoma, and Father John had gotten to know him by virtue of a coin toss. He might just as easily have ended up at the other man's place if heads hadn't come up when he had been trying to decide who should alter several pairs of his pants. It was only a couple of years ago after he actually met the tailor that he learned his first name: George. He had been told to call him Googie. The yellow pages had identified him simply as *Gilden the tailor.* Much later Father John chanced upon a *George* Gilden in the White Pages. Googie was coy about his nickname and loved to lead people on about his real name was, and how he had gotten his moniker.

"You don't think David Folkenflik or Ari Schapiro aren't Jewish like me? Or Ira Flatow, either?"

"They probably are, Googie. But Lourdes Garcia-Navarro surely isn't. Now there's a really Catholic name, Lourdes! I've only known two other women besides the lady on NPR who had that first name, by the way. You know about Lourdes in France, I assume, about the healing that goes on there starting with appearances of the Blessed Virgin to Bernadette Soubirous a hundred and sixty years ago or more."

"She doesn't count," Googie said with a big grin. "Or Lakshmi Singh, either." Another grin. "But Maura Liasson does for all I know, so does Daniel Zwerdling. And how's this for a name, especially one for a man? Sonari Glinton. Only a Jew would name his son Sonari, I think."

16

"Could be an Arab name, Googie. Wouldn't that just frost you?"

"So look who thinks he's such an expert on Jewish names now! You don't think anyone named Glinton would be Muslim, do you?"

"Perhaps not. But what if it's an African-American name, Googie? I'm just saying it could be. Surely you must agree that it *could* be. Anyway, John Zarroli certainly doesn't sound Jewish, or Mandalit del Barco. Or, for that matter, Shankar Vedantam." Father John wasn't going to be outdone. "I'll call it a draw, though, with Michele Keleman. If that name isn't German, it *could* be Jewish. You sure you're not the agent for one or more of those on-air people, Googie?"

The conversation could have gone on endlessly had Googie not called a truce to suggest a sip of wine.

Father John treasured any time he could spend with his relatively recent friend. He hoped this octogenarian pup-licker would be around a long time more. He had such fun with him every time he found an excuse to visit. In large part that was because Googie had such a quick wit and so enjoyed bantering. And there wasn't a mean bone in his body.

Father John had taken to waking at 6 to the news on NPR. Often remaining in bed until 7, he trusted a separate alarm to rouse him in case he fell back to sleep. He'd have time to perform his morning ablutions, start the coffeemaker, get the morning paper and still be on time for 8:30 Mass, even if he did occasionally puzzle over things like unusual names on the airwaves of NPR.

So it was that he found himself retrieving the Post-Dispatch at 8:10 that morning and trying to decide whether to preach a short homily a few minutes hence. As he opened the paper on the way back into the rectory, another cryptic puzzle message was tucked in among the paper's pages. This one read: *I'M COMING.*

The previous messages had been: *INTRIGUED ... YOU SHOULD BE ... and YOU'RE IT.* And now this! What in heaven's name was it all about? If it was a practical joke, it was no longer funny. He hadn't time enough to ponder it before Mass, however, so he put the paper on the kitchen table and went over to church.

Afterward, he enjoyed his coffee with some oatmeal and a piece of toast while mulling over this latest of the crossword messages. But he could make no sense of it other than that it was sounding increasingly ominous. He decided to call his friend, the sheriff. A quick check of his calendar showed him relatively free that day, so instead of calling Lawrence Toler, he decided to drive to the jail and talk to him face to face, which he did right after putting his dishes in the sink.

He found the lanky and often-laconic lawman sprawled behind his desk poring over several wanted posters. The sheriff looked up in surprise.

"What brings you here, Father? There aren't any prisoners to visit. Are you wanting to talk about my soul or those of my deputies?" He grinned.

"Nothing like that. Actually, *I* may have some business for *you*."

The sheriff's eyes sparkled with curiosity. "You don't say."

It took Father John just a couple of minutes to describe the four troubling notes he had found in his daily copies of the Post-Dispatch.

"You worried about these?"

"Wouldn't you be, Sheriff?"

"Not necessarily."

Father John then apprised him of the newly minted crossword puzzles with their link to mysteries that had recently run in the Post. "Shortly after they were introduced, St. Louis actually suffered a crossword puzzle crime, Sheriff. We could have a copycat here."

"I see what you mean. Perhaps you're onto something at that."

"I can't figure out whether it represents something serious. But I'm worried that it could be."

"Are you the only one getting these things, Father?"

"So far as I know, yes. I take it, then, that you haven't heard anything like this with regard to anyone else?"

"Correct, I haven't. But I don't have any bright ideas for you, either, other than to wait and see where this goes."

"I was hoping you might be able to do something. Like check with the paper distribution agency or mount some kind of surveillance … a camera to watch my mailbox, maybe … something like that."

"Father, you know how small our department is. We couldn't afford cameras or the like, especially for something as iffy as this.

19

And I'm not sure that if we could we'd be able to hide them well enough to keep from scaring off any perpetrator. But what I can do is check with the St. Louis PD and see if there's anything they can share that might be of help."

"Could you also run a squad car past my place between the time the paper person drops my paper off and say eight o'clock? You just might see someone or something."

"That would be pretty much a long shot, Father. But I don't think it's out of the question. My men are out and about that early, and I could have one of them swing past. But I wouldn't hold my breath as to how successful that'll be."

"Nonetheless, I'd appreciate it. And will you also let me know if anything from St. Louis turns out to be useful?"

"Be glad to. And you keep me posted if there's anything new on your end too, okay?"

CHAPTER 5

No cryptic message appeared in his paper box the next day, so after Mass Father John went looking for Maisie Brown at the bank to tell her not to clean the rectory Saturday. It was still next to impossible to get to her by phone, and Father John had given up trying to persuade her that phones weren't some kind of enemy.

She agreed to wait a week for that chore but seemed put out. Perhaps she needed the money. He'd check on that the next time she came to his place, though he wasn't sure what to do about it other than apologize for any inconvenience he may have caused her. Her financial situation was probably tenuous, though he had never delved into that, considering it too personal.

On his way out of the bank he waved to Bobbie Sue Langley. "Tell Mr. Lanner hello," he shouted at her. The bank president's personal assistant flashed him a thumbs up to indicate she would.

He hadn't been to the Langley's for a backyard barbeque that past summer, he realized, and made a mental note to ask whether they were planning something like that while the weather was still nice. He enjoyed their company and knew they enjoyed his. It wouldn't be embarrassing to invite himself to their home like that, although he could bring a salad as his contribution to the table.

When he got back home, the parish secretary was counting the Sunday collection. Coming in just twice a week, Betty had a regular routine of combining that with preparing a draft of next week's bulletin. She'd be back in two days to finalize it and run off copies. She greeted Father John cheerily and told him to call the sheriff.

"Hope everything's fine, Betty. You're sounding chipper." She smiled and nodded without skipping a beat with her tallying.

The sheriff answered the call but was noncommittal about what he wanted to discuss, insisting instead that the discussion take place at the jail and not on the phone. So Father John got back into his still-warm Taurus and headed to the jail.

"What's so secretive, Lawrence," Father John asked jovially.

"I think we need to talk about fingerprints, Father. And I don't want to take the chance of bringing that up in any way that might leak the idea to people beyond you and me."

"You think those notes still have usable fingerprints?"

"Certainly not. But I want to dust any future ones for prints. And I'm going to tell you how we'll go about that. Like your idea of 'staking out' your mailbox, this is a long shot. But it's worth a try, and if we're going to do it, we need to do it right."

"So what do you want me to do?"

"It'll be something of an inconvenience, but you'll need to wear gloves to pick up your paper each morning. We'll dust the next note plus the newspaper for prints. I'll find some pretext to talk to your paper carrier and get his prints so we can exclude him as a suspect. Any others we lift off the paper or crossword notes can be run against the FBI database.

"No need to contact me until another note shows up, but when that happens I need you to very carefully keep the paper with its notes safe from being handled by anyone. Then I'll come right over. Do you understand what I'm asking of you?"

"I think so. This strikes me as a good idea, Sheriff. But if this guy is as cagey as he seems to be so far, don't you think he'll be careful not to leave any prints?"

"We can only hope he won't have thought of that or else gets careless on a given day he leaves something for you."

"I don't know who might be able to see me get my paper, but won't it look weird my going out there with gloves on? It's hardly cold enough to merit that and will surely look strange."

"That's why I'm giving you these rubber gloves. They're like the ones doctors wear. Using latex gloves won't make your hands look suspicious. At a distance, no one should notice. Use a different pair each morning, but be sure to keep them on until after you bring the paper inside the rectory when the next note shows up. Also, try not to disturb the position of the note inside the paper. Just call me immediately before taking off those gloves, and wait 'til I get there. That should give us our best shot at finding something. Is all that clear?"

"Yes. Seems like you've thought of everything."

"I hope so. It's what I'm paid to do."

"Thanks, Sheriff."

As he drove back to the rectory, Father John stared at the box of gloves on the seat beside him. He couldn't help thinking that this was getting complicated.

CHAPTER 6

A week went by with hit-and-miss surveillance of Father John's newspaper box, during the last part of which the sheriff had begun using unmarked cars, but nothing suspicious had been noticed. On day eight, however, the culprit slipped beneath the radar and left another crossword note: *FOR YOU*.

Father John now became very concerned. Why had these notes been targeting him? He called Sheriff Toler's office immediately about the new note but had to leave a message, as the lawman hadn't arrived yet. He asked that his call be returned after his morning Mass, and promptly at 9 o'clock the rectory phone rang.

"I'll be right over. Sorry I wasn't here when you called. I trust no one has handled the paper other than yourself."

"Correct. It's waiting for you in pristine condition, so to speak, on my kitchen table. I sure hope there are some prints. Other than the paper carrier's, I mean."

Several minutes later, the be-gloved sheriff scooped up both items and promised to call as soon as anything came back from the FBI. Unfortunately, that search yielded only the delivery person's prints. The sheriff decided to continue the surveillance nonetheless, though he admitted that this now seemed an even longer shot than before.

Father John told himself that he had gotten his hopes up too high but still couldn't shake his disappointment with things as they now stood. And he was more certain than ever that someone was playing very unfriendly mind games with him.

It's a conspiracy!

No sooner than that occurred to him did he think of the young men in town who had been targeted by a conspiracy the previous spring. Perhaps he could somehow enlist their aid. Until then he hadn't mentioned the notes or how much they had begun to worry him to anyone but the sheriff. But the young fellows, especially Jim Eisner, were another matter. While he wasn't sure how they might help, he knew he could trust them and thought it worth a try.

He phoned Jim at work and asked him to stop at the rectory on his way home that evening. He didn't volunteer any particulars, and Jim didn't ask for any. *It shouldn't take too long,* he had told him.

When they met a little after five in the rectory kitchen, Jim asked eagerly: "What's up, Father?"

"Well, I have a complicated and perhaps lengthy story to tell you. Do you have time? Might you need to call home about supper?"

"How long do think it'll take, Father?"

"Not sure, but I'd say no more than twenty minutes. Is that okay?"

"Should be. May I use your phone."

Father John was soon explaining the crossword puzzle game that the Post-Dispatch had begun some weeks earlier and the surprising discovery by the St. Louis police shortly afterward of an actual crime committed emulating that game.

"A little after that, I started getting similar clues tucked into my copy of the Post. They haven't come every day, but over a period of several weeks I've gotten the following messages in this order: Intrigued ... you should be ... you are it ... I'm coming ... for you."

"Do you think they're serious?"

"Yes, and I've enlisted the aid of the sheriff, who also thinks they could be serious. To be on the safe side he's been sending squad cars at random times past the rectory of an early morning, but so far no one has been spotted planting those notes. And the most recent one was dusted for fingerprints, but so far nothing useful has turned up on that, either."

"Have you told anyone else about this, Father?"

"No, until you. Nor have I told the sheriff that I'm letting you in on it, but I'll do that tomorrow, whether you sign onto the project or not. He wants to know exactly who's in the know. I'm not sure exactly how you and your friends can help, but I figured that the five of you who were targeted last spring by Gil Wetzel would at least understand how this feels and could be another set of eyes and ears for me on this."

"You want us to keep watch on your paper box?"

"No. There's no good way to do that. And anyway that'd be asking way too much, even if you divvied that up among you. I was thinking more along the lines of your keeping alert around town for anything new and different — suspicious, you know. It's a long shot, but it can't hurt. You'll need to be discreet, of course, but I'm hoping you can manage that."

"Well, I'm game. And as a matter of fact, Father, our group has taken to gathering on Saturday mornings at McDonald;s. You know we did that to put together our experiences involving that skeleton in the woods from back when we were kids. We met then at the truck stop, but nowadays we just get together at McDonald's for a guys-morning-out to share gossip and family goings-on … stuff like that. We like it that last spring's grizzly business brought us boyhood friends back together again, and we've decided to keep that up, at least for the time being. It'll be easy on Saturday to ask them to be your eyes and ears around here. With a bit of luck we'll stumble onto something."

"Unless you think changing your pattern might look strange, you might want to go back to the truck stop. They do a great breakfast, I guess you know."

"It could look strange, as you say. And anyway, we don't eat anything. We just have coffee. I think we'll stick with our established routine. Besides, some of the old farts in town now hang out at the truck stop. For some reason they switched from McDonald's, so we've got more privacy now."

"I understand. Do you think they'll want to help?"

"Pretty sure, yes. Every so often they still speak of how grateful they are about your help last spring. One thing, though: I think you should not be part of our gathering next Saturday. Your presence might cause undue curiosity among any hangers-on at the restaurant."

"Oh, I agree. But if at some time the group might want more details than you're able to provide, Jim, I'd be glad to supply those. I imagine that could be done here in the rectory without attracting undue attention, since all of you are Catholic. But I agree that it's best not to involve me in such a public place. Besides, if I were there, it might put too much pressure to get involved on those who might not want to."

"Well, tell the sheriff tomorrow, then. And if he doesn't like the idea, there's still time to tell me not to bring it up on Saturday."

Father John felt a good deal of relief after Jim left. He'd call Sheriff Toler after Mass in the morning.

CHAPTER 7

On Saturday at McDonald's, Jim Eisner hung back from the conversation, looking for the right time to mention Father John.

The group sometimes skipped a Saturday when not enough of them could make it, and on any given Saturday morning not every one of them might be there. But that day all five were there, which would make it an ideal time for Jim's message.

Rick Binz dominated the conversation at first, regaling the group with an extended tale about his mother-in-law's recent visit. He had them laughing at his spin on the antics of his wife's mother whom he actually liked, although he portrayed her in his tale as a stereotypic meddler.

Tom Bigger had nothing to contribute but was eagerly egging Rick on. And Paul Leubel and Harry Grant were laughing too much to be able to be add anything, so Jim spoke up about his recent conversation with Father Wintermann during the lull at the end of Rick's story.

Once they heard Father John's name, the group immediately focused intently on what Jim had to say about the past several weeks in their pastor's life, and when he finished with a request to join him in assisting their pastor, the four immediately chimed in affirmatively.

Rick wanted to know exactly how they could help.

"Just keep your eyes and ears open for anything out of the ordinary in town. New people, changes in patterns, loose talk … that kind of stuff. But he wants us to keep quiet about what we're up to. Nothing about Father John or these notes he's been getting."

Tom volunteered: "Well, there have been several people moving away from town recently, but I don't guess that's much help."

"Anybody new with us here?" Jim wanted to know.

"The Dudenbostel family moved in near me," Paul said.

"The who?" Jim asked. "You sure you got their name right? That sounds like something from a comedy sketch. Dudenbostel?"

"Yeah, I thought so too, but that's the name, all right," Paul answered. "I did a double-take when they introduced themselves, and they laughed off my questioning it. They get that all the time, they said."

"What he's do?" Harry asked. "I don't think he works in town. And what are their first names, anyway?"

"He's Herman and works at Scott Field, Harry; pretty high up in the pecking order over there, according to him. He works directly under the Number One civilian guy in administration. A few of his relatives had come from Algoma, or at least nearby … some time ago, I think. I didn't get his wife's first name."

"How long ago?" Jim asked. "The name's not familiar. And with a name like that, it oughtta be."

"Not sure," Paul said. But I can ask. Want me to?"

"Sure," Jim said, "but don't make it sound too obvious. Find a good time. Who knows, that might be important."

"I can't imagine that they're up to anything with Father John. How could you get by with anything shady sporting a name like that?"

They all laughed.

"Anybody got anything else that comes to mind right now?"

Jim got no takers, so they finished their coffee with Jim reminding them about keeping this hush-hush. "If you get anything, tell me right away, but don't use the phone or write anything down. Come past my house or meet me somewhere. Okay?"

Afterward, Jim stopped at the rectory to briefly report to Father John, who asked if the Dudenbostels were Catholics. Jim didn't know, but promised to get back to him when he found out. Father John said he hadn't heard about them until that moment and mumbled aloud that he wouldn't try to visit them just yet. But if they were Catholic …

Before that afternoon's Mass, Father John made a mental note to stop at the Becker pharmacy on Monday to see what they knew about the new family.

He was relieved that now there were some new wheels in motion.

CHAPTER 8

The Beckers didn't know the Dudenbostels, let alone the religion they practiced. But Father John had a delightful conversation anyway with Fred and Frieda despite their being busy with customers all afternoon. He'd talk to whichever of them was free at the moment, knowing that the message would be relayed to the missing spouse. He was able to tell them that the Dudenbostels were new in town and that he hoped the Beckers would get their business. Having only one pharmacy in town didn't necessarily cinch that; some folks went to Burger for their drugs.

The chat lasted surprisingly long because of the customer interruptions, and Father John learned that Scott Field had recently begun a civilian hiring surge because of the transfer of another Air Command into that facility. Fred thought that might explain why someone like Mr. Dudenbostel was hired recently.

"Makes sense to me," Father John said.

After he left the pharmacy, Father John drove to Burger to visit patients at Saint Luke's hospital and then went home. As he drove into his driveway in the late afternoon, he noticed something sticking out of the Post-Dispatch box. It was another of the crossword notes. He was surprised at the change in procedure and wondered if the perp, as Sheriff Toler had taken to calling the person leaving the notes, had somehow got wind of the efforts to catch him in the act. He was glad he remembered to pick up the paper with his handkerchief.

Once inside the rectory he called the sheriff and read the clue aloud for him: *BUT WHEN*. Obviously this was meant to bedevil Father John. He even smiled as he realized the strategy was working. The sheriff came ten minutes later and collected the newest piece of evidence and was assured that Father John hadn't left his own prints on it. But several days later, the FBI once again confirmed that this latest clue had no prints on it.

The young men didn't have anything new to offer over the next two weeks, during which time there were also no new notes. Father John put the matter onto the back burner of his awareness when Jim Eisner called to tell him that four new families had moved into Algoma, all of them recently hired at Scott Field. He said he'd have more about them soon, and Father John urged him to tell Sheriff Toler that along with any developments with those families. But that proved in time to have no significance that any of the young men, Father John or the sheriff could determine.

Nothing seemed to be working, and Father John felt a new wave of disappointment. He had been careful from the beginning not to let on anything to his parishioners or the citizens of Algoma, but he couldn't be sure that whoever was planting those notes hadn't noticed something. He kept telling himself to look cool, even if he didn't feel that way.

A month went by since Jim and his friends promised their help. It was already October, and in the meantime another note appeared once again in the morning: *NOT YET*. It appeared that the person leaving the notes was deliberately trying to push Father John into more and more frustration. Indeed, the strategy was close to working. While Father John got more and more data from the mysterious notes, he was no closer than ever to deciphering their ultimate meaning, and he ping-ponged between frustration, anger and bemusement.

Then one morning after Mass he got an idea and quickly shared it with the sheriff. What if he sent a letter for publication in the Post to its crossword editor about his getting those clues? That might help flush out the perp, the sheriff said, warning him not to put his name on the letter. Father John disagreed lest the editor not accept it, but he could request it be printed with the disclaimer that the name was withheld by mutual agreement. That way only the perp would know who had actually written it.

It was agreed, and the letter went out the next day. Within two days Father John got a call from the Post that it would appear in two days. Father John began feeling some hope again. Surely the perp couldn't resist responding to a provocation like that.

The letter's appearance brought no response for several days. Then a phone message was left on the rectory's answering machine during morning Mass. Father John surmised that the guy knew he wouldn't be in then and a message could be left without running the risk of giving himself away via a live conversation.

The recorded message was pointedly brief, cryptic and maddening. A deliberately disguised male voice said: *THEY'RE CROSS WORDS*! Caller ID provided a number the sheriff traced to a pay phone at Lambert Field in St. Louis. Again the perp had shown clever carefulness, and Father John's frustration began spiraling upward once more.

What could that possibly mean: *cross words*? The voice had very deliberately separated the word into two words. The sheriff and Father John figured it had to mean something beyond the obvious, namely that the notes were in the form of crossword answers. But what?

Father John mulled over all the possibilities he could come up with: cross, meaning angry; cross with religious overtones; cross meaning crossword, thus indicating more to play out as the puzzle expanded …

Perhaps he should put them into the shape of a cross or crosses and some new meaning would be revealed. So he attempted to construct something like that with as many of the permutations as he could assemble. But nothing with any clarity emerged. Father John decided to give it a rest and come back to it a few days later. Maybe by then something might make sense.

Meantime, he decided he had better concentrate more on his parishioners. Perhaps some home visits might be not only productive ministerially but would also serve to get his mind off those darned crossword clues. He decided to visit Lumpy Wurtz and bring along a couple of steaks. After a stop at Hy's grocery store, with steaks in hand, he drove his Taurus out into the country to the man's farm, where he found Lumpy puttering around in one of his outbuildings.

"What brings you out here, Father?"

"I hadn't seen you in a long while and haven't had a good steak lately, either. Two birds with one stone, don't you know," he said, brandishing the package of meat overhead as he approached the shed.

Lumpy beamed. "I need a break myself. Glad to see you. I couldn't decide if I wanted to pull some bluegill out of the freezer or some of my beef. Now there's no need for a decision." He grinned again. "As much as I like bluegill, beef trumps fish any day."

As they headed into the house, Father John volunteered to oversee the baking of a couple of potatoes.

"Nah. I'll put 'em on the grill and add the steaks later. Let's see what we've got for veggies or a salad." A few discovered carrots and some frozen green beans would do nicely, they decided, and Father John got busy getting them ready while he encouraged Richard — Lumpy's real name and the only name Father John ever used when talking to or about him — to tell him about the goings-on in his life.

"Mostly the same old same old, Father, except I took a couple of cows to slaughter. Got decent prices, too. Another one is in my freezer now, so you wouldn't really have had to bring those steaks. But Hy's meat is great — don't get me wrong. I'm not complaining none about your generosity. Just don't bother with that next time."

Father John took that for humor, except his friend's face kept its serious demeanor. Sometimes he couldn't tell if Richard was joshing him or not. But it didn't matter. He enjoyed his farmer friend so much, and the chemistry between them was so good, that neither felt obliged to laugh at the other's whimsy.

36

Lumpy went on and on about his same old same old, which Father John never found boring. The conversation lasted into supper and beyond, ranging over everything from the herd to plans for fixing up an outbuilding or two — their roofs needed work, his host had decided.

It had gotten dark by the time Father John reluctantly said he should be getting back to town. The men rose silently from the swing on the front porch where they had ended up after doing the dishes, and Father John smiled at his friend as he bade him goodbye.

By the time he got home, Father John was feeling tired, the result of the nice meal and a little wine. He swung into his driveway and couldn't resist looking, but nothing new was poking out of his paper box, so once inside he checked messages and went to bed. His spur-of-the-moment visit had been a good thing. He'd have to do more of that and get back into the swing of ministry to his Saint Helena's pup-lickers.

CHAPTER 9

Lumpy Wurtz called a couple of days later. "Surprised to hear from me so soon? I know we just got together, Father, but I enjoyed that so much that I want you to come out again.

"Hello, Richard. What a great idea. When would be good?"

"Well I don't know if you realize it, but Mrs. Hennessy is laid up with something or other and can't get to church."

"I should have checked when I missed her last weekend, but I thought she might be visiting relatives. What's the matter with her?"

"Don't know for sure, but Lottie Grimm told me yesterday that she'd brought some soup over to her. I thought you'd want to know about her incapacitation. And I thought that maybe you could kill two birds with one stone and come my way as well."

"You know I want that kind of information about my flock, Richard. Thanks for letting me know. On my way to her place, I could bring another steak or two from Hy's market so's we can spend another evening together over a nice meal."

"I rarely turn down offers like that. But remember what I said: no need for that. When you thinkin' of seein' Bessie?" he drawled. "In a day or two?"

"Today, if I can get something good at Hy's. I need something for myself. Don't worry, I won't bring anything out your way. I'll give you a call to let you know for sure when I'll be able to arrive."

"I'll wait to hear. And tell Bessie hi for me."

When he hung up, Father John made a list of people he ought to contact for a home visit. Meantime, he picked up the phone and gave Bessie Hennessy a call. With any luck, he could be out to see her within an hour, even if he spent a few minutes more on that list.

Bessie was grateful to hear from her pastor and said she only had a bad cold. But he could come anyway. She might even brew some tea. Then he called Lumpy to confirm that he'd be there soon.

His list completed, he backed out of the garage and glanced at his paper box on his way out of the driveway. He was surprised to see something there. It had to have appeared within the past couple of hours. Perhaps it was just a note from a parishioner. He stopped to retrieve it. But it was no note. It was another crossword clue: NOT YET.

The discovery upset him, and he had to take a couple of minutes as his car idled in the driveway to regain his composure. By the time he set out he was calm again. He realized there was nothing he could do about getting another clue, but he'd make sure the sheriff heard about it when he got to Bessie's place. Why was he so upset, he wondered. He finally decided that it was the brazenness of the fellow: broad daylight for goodness sake, and not the first time, at that!

The clue didn't help him unravel anything. The previous clue had said **WHEN**. And now: *NOT YET*. So? Nothing new, really, which was disappointing. *He's toying with me again!*

That upset him further, but he knew that if he gave into feelings like that, he was only allowing the perp to win psychologically. Still, it irked him. He had sat for a few minutes to clear away those feelings. He didn't want them to frustrate his visit with Bessie or with Richard, either.

Hy was swamped with customers at the meat counter, so Father John had to settle for the two nicely marbled steaks and a quick thank-you to the grocer before returning to the front of the store. And Jimmy, Hy's cashier, was his usual business-only self: nothing but the words needed for the moment, no matter what Father John tried — and he had tried numerous times before. He wasn't sure, but he thought Jimmy was from Burger. He certainly didn't attend Saint Helena's.

On his way out of town after putting the steaks into his refrigerator, he spied Horace Denver in an alley and wheeled his Taurus into the next several right turns to catch up with the junk man before he got away from the Turner home.

"Horace, I haven't talked with you in too long a while. I hope everything's fine. You never stay after church to chat, so I have to resort to tracking you down." He smiled at the junk man and was rewarded with a grin from the reticent son of Annie Verden, a genealogical fact known to Father John and only one other man in town, the banker, Bob Lanner.

"How are you, Father?"

"I'm doing well. But, if you don't mind, I'd like a favor. I've been getting unsigned notes stuffed into my Post-Dispatch box. Have you ever seen anyone putting something there?" He could trust Horace not to spread that around. The man talked so little and to very few people, besides.

"Nope, sure haven't. Want me to keep watch on it?"

"Yes, if you can do that without attracting much attention. Don't want to scare the person off. Who knows, you might see something. If so, let me know, please, especially if you know who it is."

"Sure. But what if I don't know the person?

"Well, I suppose you could describe him, and perhaps his vehicle too. Maybe even get a license number."

"Be glad to. It'll be like solving a mystery, won't it?"

"More than you know, Horace. And thanks." They exchanged waves as Horace preceded Father John out of the alley.

Minutes later he was out of town and enjoying the autumn countryside on his way to another much anticipated visit with his old friend. A bottle of Cabernet was safely beside him, and he knew there would be beer at the farm for snacks and conversation before the meal. The wine would complement the steak. But first: Bessie.

The older woman was happy to see him and claimed he shouldn't have troubled himself over just a cold. But he knew she would be pleased, and his gift of Holy Communion was icing on the cake. Father John was glad he could spend time with her whether she brewed some of her special herbal tea or not. And he was grateful to farmer Wurtz for alerting him. He wished more people in the parish would do that. It would make his ministry more complete, not to mention more satisfying.

He left the Hennessy farm and was finally able to turn his attention to his friend. He found Richard standing on his porch as he drove up. He disappeared inside briefly but was back outside by the time Father John got out of his car and was awaiting him with two beers in hand. There was also a plate of sausage and crackers on the table between the two wicker porch chairs, and the two men sat down to watch the evening approach so they could, as they often put it, tell lies while settling world problems.

"Have you ever been to the horseradish festival in Collinsville?"

"What brings that up, Richard?"

"I just got some really good, really strong, horseradish to replace what I got in Collinsville this summer. It'll go great with the steak."

"Can't say as I have, but I've heard of it. It's one of those things I'd like to do sometime. Do you go often?"

"Every other year or so. I enjoy it. There's wonderful stuff there, and some surprising things, like horseradish ice cream."

"You're kidding."

"Nope. And it's surprisingly good.

"When is it?"

"Early June."

"Well, I certainly couldn't have done it this year, even if I'd been aware of it. That was when those young men got caught up in that conspiracy, and we had way too many funerals … which then pushed me into that trip to the Northwest for what turned out to be a wonderful retreat with the Benedictines in Washington. But what about next year? Might you be going to that festival then?"

"I could. Would you tag along?"

"I wouldn't go on my own … but with someone who knows the ropes, why, I'd love to spend a day there. And it's not that far."

"Consider it a deal. I'll warn you ahead of time. That shindig's on a weekend, so I suppose you'll want to go Friday afternoon … or maybe after Sunday Mass. We'd have more time then."

"Sunday it is, then. Be sure to remind me."

"You can count on it."

Late afternoon morphed into evening, and Richard finally rose to start the fire on his grill. Steak, potatoes and some roasted squash made for a wonderful repast, and both men agreed that there was no need for dessert. "That's fortunate, because I don't have any," Lumpy grinned.

When Father John left, after giving the wine time enough to render him safe from a possible DUI, it was well into a beautiful drive home by the light of a full moon. *I won't wait that long before repeating this*, he mused. *Richard's too special and this was great fun.*

CHAPTER 10

The next morning when Father John looked out his bedroom window, he couldn't believe his eyes. He hadn't paid attention to the weather forecast and was surprised to see a light blanket of snow.

He generally liked snowfalls, at least when they didn't hinder travel or become a problem for older people getting around on town sidewalks, so today's light snow cover pleased him, and he found himself humming as he went about his morning routine. As he looked out from his back door before going to get his paper, he spotted footprints in the snow leading from what looked like undisturbed tire tracks to his newspaper box and instantly realized there might finally be a breakthrough with regard to the crossword clues.

He immediately called the sheriff at his home to tell him the news. "I haven't disturbed the area out there, Sheriff. I thought you might be able to find out something from the footprints."

"Perhaps, but we might get even luckier with the tire tracks. I'll have someone get there pronto to take castings of both sets of prints. Why don't you position yourself so's to scare off anyone before my deputy gets there? Don't want anyone messin' up the crime scene."

"Will that be soon, Sheriff? I have Mass in half an hour."

"Should be just a few minutes," Sheriff Toler said and hung up.

True to the sheriff's word, a deputy showed up fifteen minutes later and Father John hollered out to him that no one had disturbed the scene. He could hardly contain his curiosity during Mass about what this stroke of luck might lead to. His call to the jail after Mass resulted in an invitation to join the sheriff as soon as he could. He was out the door immediately after hanging up the phone.

"When you think about it," Father John said as soon as he entered the sheriff's office, "I find it strange that this fellow who's been so careful not to leave any clues to his identity would be so careless as to leave another note when tracks in the snow could give him away." Both men were by then looking at the latest note: *SOON*.

"Did you get anything useful from the two sets of prints?" Father John wanted to know.

"We got very good impressions from the footprints and the tire tracks, Father, but it remains to be seen how useful they'll be. I can tell you the size of the man's foot — and it almost certainly is a man, judging from the size and the kind of tread. The sole pattern probably won't help us much. It looks too common. It comes from a work shoe or boot. But the size might in time be helpful. The guy wears an 11. So he's probably a big man. And the depth of the footprints in the snow also points to that.

"As to the tire tracks, they're more helpful. They come from an SUV, and almost certainly a Dodge. We're looking through the state registry to see if there are any vehicles like that in our area. I'll let you know if and when we find something on that.

"I agree with you. It does seem like our guy dropped the ball and got careless. In any case, we got lucky, I think. This freaky snowstorm as well as his carelessness! Who knew?"

"How long before you find out something on the car, Sheriff?"

"Might be a few days. I'll be in touch. Try not to worry about it. It'll come when it comes, Padre."

"I feel a whole lot better with all this breaking. Can't wait to hear back from you."

By the time he returned to the rectory, Father John noticed the snow had already begun to melt. *We really did get lucky!*

By the next day, Indian summer had returned and the snow was a completely faded memory. The crossword clue itself didn't give even a substantive hint as to what the game was all about. All it did was prolong the agony ... again. Father John was just being strung along, he felt, and it was beginning to make him angry.

The sheriff called a day later to say that, as he had feared, there were hundreds of Dodge SUVs in the state and more than twenty within twenty-five miles of Algoma. He was tracking them all down but admitted that even if he could narrow the list down to a manageable few, there would be little he could use to even bring someone in for questioning. "Unless, which is unlikely, it's a truly unique tire print." But it *was* progress.

When Father John put his phone back onto its cradle, he wasn't so sure he agreed. *It doesn't feel like progress. I should have asked if any of those cars belonged to people here in Algoma.* He didn't feel like bothering the sheriff by calling back. *I'll ask the next time we talk. Hope I remember to do that.*

The rest of the week proceeded more or less routinely for the pastor of Saint Helena's. The bulletin was prepared, his homily finalized, several people were visited at the Burger hospital … and no more clues appeared. It would take, in fact, almost two more weeks for that to happen … more time spent by Father John in mostly nervous waiting. *Perhaps that's the strategy: bedevil me, string me along, have fun at my expense. What if all this is nothing more than some sadist's mind game … someone who doesn't like me or my parish?*

He couldn't be sure, of course.

But he realized he was already being bugged by it.

CHAPTER 11

He wasn't sure where the idea came from. It was just there one morning when he woke up, and having no pressing matters to attend to that day, Father John decided to act on it. He'd go to the courthouse to see if he could find the Dudenbostel name in the county records. It just didn't seem right that while that family was Catholic — at least that's what he had been told — they didn't attend Saint Helena's. One of the young men he had sniffing around for leads on the crossword clues thought the family had roots in Algoma but that they were going to Burger for church. Father John hoped to find something he could use to bring them back to where he felt they belonged.

As he entered the courthouse, he ran into Pat Kelly.

"Long time no see, Pat. How are you doing?"

"Fine, Father. Busy. But that's good."

"Busy with what? Anything spectacular?"

"A lot of in-office stuff: wills, probate work ... you know: stuff like that. Why? Got something juicy for me to relieve the boredom?"

"Can't say as I do, Pat, but it would be nice to work with you again. Given your connection with Annie Verden and her Pittsburgh nephews, do you still have anything to do with the beneficiaries of her estate?" He hesitated to use any names because he couldn't remember if Bob Lanner was in the will, and he didn't want to open a can of worms by mentioning Horace Denver.

"No, that's all old news, I'm afraid. But what brings you to the hallowed halls of justice today, Father?"

"Going to scrounge around in the records to see if a new family in town had any connections to Algoma way back when."

"May I ask who?"

"Not sure you'd know them, Pat. The Dudenbostel family."

"Did I hear you right? Dudenbostel? That's a mouthful. I think I might change my name if I were born with that."

"So you've not heard about these new arrivals to our fair city?"

"Like what?"

"A family with that name moved here not long ago, and with a name like that, my curiosity's been sparked. I'm off on a name safari in this building's most ancient tomes. Just in case."

"In case of what?"

"In case I can find something to pleasantly surprise them with if or when I make a pastoral visit to their home. It's always good to be prepared. Some tidbit like that could work wonders establishing rapport when you first meet someone. At least I find that helpful in my profession. And since today is a pretty slow one — in fact, this whole week looks that way right now — I thought I'd indulge my curiosity and spend time in our venerable archives, dark and mysterious as they might seem ... sort of like the Dark Continent Africa, you know. Hence my calling it a safari." He was mildly pleased with himself over that allusion.

"Lawyering affords me enough research that I'd consider it a busman's holiday at best. You're welcome to it. I'm not even tempted to come look over your shoulder."

"I understand. Anyway, you'd just be in the way." He grinned at his friend and, with a gentle wave, took off down the corridor.

"Are you up for lunch some time soon?" Pat asked as his pastor took off.

"Always up for that," the priest said over his shoulder. "Thanks for the offer. Call me. I might even go Dutch and save you from tacking that cost onto some client's bill." He chuckled quietly.

"Just so you don't take the cost out of some slush fund for candles or something, Father." *Touche,* Kelly thought and grinned.

Happy not to have let the lawyer see it, so did Father John, but he continued on his way without further comment.

Several hours later he had yet to meet with any success in his search and was feeling somewhere between bored and disappointed. He thought he was probably not very efficient in his search methods. There were no obvious shortcuts, so he had simply started at the chronological beginning of the county's records and was slowly plowing through the registered births and deaths. He had gotten to the mid-1800s without finding one mention of Dudenbostel.

Marriage records might be next once he got into the twentieth century with his current search. And there were also census records to consider, but he wasn't sure where they could be found. So far this was proving to be a boring slog through county history.

When he finally gave up, his energy and enthusiasm were flagging. But he remained determined to see the project through. He just wasn't sure how soon he wanted to return for round two.

CHAPTER 12

There hadn't been a funeral at Saint Helena's since early summer, at which time he had judged there had been too many, given the deaths of those young men then. But there would be be one within the week, as Father John learned next morning from one of the Feldspar brothers who told him of the death of a former parishioner in the desert Southwest.

"Maryanne Grimmlesman had a heart attack early today, Father. Do you remember her?"

"Indeed I do. After the death of her husband a few years ago, she left Algoma to live in … Phoenix or Tucson, I forget which."

"Tucson, Father. The family wants the funeral here at Saint Helena's, as you might guess. We'll have to await shipment of the body, of course, but we should be able to have the service at the end of the week, if that works for you. Saturday okay?"

"Certainly, Larry. What time? The usual?"

"Yes, ten o'clock shouldn't be a problem."

"And the rosary the night before? At seven?"

"Most probably, but I haven't finalized everything with the family. I'll get back to you."

"And you'll get funeral cards to the businesses in town?"

"Of course."

"Can I at least announce the funeral at daily Mass the rest of this week?"

"Yes. And as soon as I know about the rosary, I'll let you know so you can announce that too."

"Good. Thanks for the call, Larry."

Father John knew this meant among other things that he'd be riding to the cemetery with Larry Feldspar Sr. He hadn't seen him since those early summer funerals and missed his good humor. No matter how sad the funeral, the ride in the hearse with Feldspar always made for tension relief. The man never failed to have a story ready. He didn't tell jokes, but his stories were unfailingly funny.

Perhaps a decade earlier the paterfamilias had stepped down from day-to-day operations at the funeral home that bore his name, and he was richly enjoying semi-retirement. Among the few tasks he held onto were driving the hearse to the cemetery and often working the front door as greeter. He knew everyone in town and provided a comforting presence as the first person they met at evening wakes.

Father John gathered his thoughts about Maryanne, his first step in preparing a funeral homily. By week's end he'd be fully ready. But moments like these became opportunities to reflect on past funerals, especially the most recent. It was his way of preserving a meaningful connection with all those who had fashioned Saint Helena's into what it was today. He saw them as links in an unbroken spiritual chain of people whom Saint Paul would undoubtedly call saints, something very important for him as a pastor. Most probably few others at Saint Helena's had that vision, and even fewer would appreciate its importance. But it was Father John's way of keeping the

Church Militant and the Church Triumphant linked together: the saints interceding on behalf of the living stones, as Paul called us here.

His reverie was broken by the sound of the rectory doorbell. *Who can that be? I'm not expecting anyone this morning.*

It turned out to be one of the five young men he had enlisted to report on town goings-on.

"Well, you're an unexpected pleasure, Harry. Come in."

Harry Grant grinned, but seemed in a hurry.

"I can't stay long, Father. Just took a quick break to come over here. I didn't want to trust this to a phone call. The others and I haven't had much to tell you 'til yesterday. And this might not even be that helpful. But for what it's worth, I noticed a new vehicle in town a week or so ago and finally found out to whom it belongs, or at least where it got parked regularly: at the Dudenbostel home. Remember? The new family in town! And it's a second car for them ... at least I never saw it 'til recently. That's probably why I couldn't pin things down about it right away. Maybe it's new. Or else they might not drive it frequently."

Father John got excited. "What kind of car is it, Harry?"

"It's one of the larger Hondas."

"You mean a van?"

"No, a large sedan. Why?"

"Oh, nothing much." He deliberately avoided the sheriff's search for an SUV. "I was thinking they perhaps had a large enough family that they'd have to haul everyone around in a van."

"No, there's no family. That is, no little kids. I suspect this is the wife's car. But I wanted you to know about it. Not sure it means anything, but it could, for all I know. So, there it is: my latest. Not much, but at least promptly reported." He smiled. "Hope it helps. Gotta get back to work now. See you, Father."

As Harry was stepping outside, the rectory phone rang. "Thanks, Harry," Father John shouted then turned to get to the phone in his office. Shirley from the chancery wanted to clarify something on a report he had recently sent in.

When he finished talking to the pleasant secretary in Belleville, he sat for several moments trying to figure if Harry's recent information had anything to do with the crossword clues, but he couldn't find any connection. So he stored the tidbit in the back of his mind. *Maybe it'll be helpful down the line. I hope* something's *helpful down the line*, he thought and smiled wryly.

Turning his efforts to tidying up his office didn't provide much peace. He couldn't get his mind off the Dudenbostels, so he decided to return to the courthouse after lunch. Then he thought of Pat Kelly. *Maybe he'd like that lunch today.*

A quick phone call confirmed his hopes. Pat would meet him at the deli on the corner across from the courthouse for an early repast at 11:15. From there it would be easy for Father John to continue his search for the Dudenbostels: just stroll across the street. Perhaps today he'd get lucky and find their county roots … or determine definitively that he was going down a blind alley.

CHAPTER 13

The meal with Pat Kelly proved too much of a temptation for Father John. He had mulled over the idea and decided that Pat's legal mind may be able to help with his crossword mystery. In no time he had Pat's undivided attention.

"Why didn't you tell me the other day that you did indeed have something juicy?"

"Well, it's been rather hush-hush between me and the sheriff … plus a few other young fellows in town who are in effect my community eyes and ears. They're trying to sniff out anything peculiar, whatever doesn't seem to ordinarily belong, you know. And the sheriff thought it best that we not let on about the SUV even to them, lest we scare off somebody. But I figure you know how to keep things quiet and might even have an angle on this that we've not thought of."

"I'll be glad to help, honored, in fact. But I suspect my assistance will most likely limit itself to legal concerns. Nonetheless, count me in."

"Who knows how your legal expertise might come into play, Pat, but I also think you could keep your eyes open like those young guys. We know there's a Dodge SUV of relatively recent vintage — that is, the past several years — that's delivered at least one of the clues. I'm not sure if there are any cars like that in Algoma … I've yet to ask the sheriff about that. But you might spot such a car here or elsewhere in the county, and you might pick up on other things too.

Anything at all could help. If you do unearth something, get back to *me*, please, not the sheriff. I'm trusting my intuition about bringing people on board to help with this mystery, and I don't know for sure how Sheriff Toler might take it if he learns the size of the group I've put my trust in."

The rest of their conversation consisted mostly of Pat's describing an interesting case from several years back in which he successfully defended a man against a rape accusation. Father John was surprised he hadn't heard of it before and listened intently to his friend's monologue.

He worked until nearly five o'clock on a fruitless search of the remaining birth and death records — those before the twentieth century — reasoning that anything after 1900 was probably too recent. Marriage records would be next when he mounted the energy for that. Census records were also possible. He had found out that he could access those online and had begun to figure that they might, after all, hold out the best possibility of success in his quest.

CHAPTER 14

Father John awoke to a report on NPR from Africa by Ofeibea Quist-Arcton and before he got out of bed forty-five minutes later there was another piece from the West Coast by Quil Lawrence. He smiled to remember his summer conversation with Father Olav at Saint Martin's Abbey about all those strange names on National Public Radio. And Googie Gilden ws also interested in that.

He could easily reprise that chat with his tailor friend because he had a pair of pants with a ripped left pocket that needed Goggie's magic. In fact, as he went about his morning ablutions he decided to go there after Mass. *But I should bring a bottle of* wine. *I think there's one left from my Christmas gifts.* Sure enough, there was one in the back of his closet. That settled it. He'd see Googie in an hour or so.

"So what, already? Still hard on your clothes?" the tailor said as he opened the door of his home from which he worked. "Great! Otherwise I'd be out of a job, and at my age, who'd take care of me?" Googie asked about the paper sack in the priest's hand.

"It's a surprise for you. A bottle of very special wine."

"If it's red, we can open it now. If it's white, you have to stay long enough to chill it briefly." The old tailor was grinning ear to ear.

"It's red, but I can't stay long. Just enough perhaps to have a sip of wine and discuss a very important matter."

"And what would that be that I should be able to help such an eminent theologian as yourself?"

"No flattery, please, Googie. Just tell me if you've heard of Ofeibea Quist-Arcton and/or Quil Lawrence?"

"Who hasn't? If you're an astute observer of the world scene you've heard of those reporters. So, what's so important that we should discuss them … or is it something they've reported on?"

"No, just their *names*. You think *they're* Jewish?"

"Heaven's no! They should be so lucky. She's British, if I don't miss my guess, and he's got to be Hispanic, maybe Italian or perhaps even Spanish. I bet you thought I wouldn't know." He was beaming.

"I'm impressed. What told you that about Lawrence? His name doesn't sound either Hispanic or Mediterranean."

"Maybe his last name doesn't, but Quil is short for Aquila, and there are only so many ethnic possibilities for that first name. His mother had to come from some hot-blooded background or other."

"And just how did you know it's short for Aquila, Googie?"

"I looked it up on my computer. You think you're the only one who can work one of those things?"

Father John laughed and accepted a glass of wine from his host. "Do you like Merlot, Googie? I was hoping you do."

"That's *my* question, since I figure you give me a bottle of it because maybe you don't want to drink it yourself."

"From anyone else I'd take that as an insult, but not from someone as cagey as you," Father John said, laughing.

The two friends spent nearly the next hour bantering and enjoying every minute. It was longer than Father John had planned,

58

but he had the benefit of walking out the door with his mended pair of pants, Googie having decided he might as well finish them while they talked. As a bonus, the tailor said the wine was payment enough for his services, which, truth to tell, didn't take all that much time.

"If I'd have known it was that easy, I'd have always brought wine, my friend … and may well do that from now on." The tailor just rolled his eyes in response.

On a whim, Father John decided to ask the older man if he knew anyone by the name of Dudenbostel.

"Now there's a name that could be Yiddish. But I'm sorry to say I don't know anybody that uses it. Why?"

"It's the name of a family that recently moved into town."

"I'd certainly remember if I'd met them. You don't hear names that exotic very often. Do they have some significance?"

"Not that I know of. I've just been curious about them because I hear they're Catholic, but they don't come to Saint Helena's."

"So you go shepherding after stray lambs, maybe?"

Father John laughed. "Something like that. But would you let me know if you hear anything? I've gotten pretty curious about them."

Googie promised to but added: "I hope they learn how precious they are. Or do you chase down every such lead with equal passion?"

Father John nodded. "It comes with the territory, Googie." Father John soon politely excused himself and rose to leave. Both were smiling when Father John waved goodbye and drove away.

With nothing else pressing that morning, Father John decided on the spur of the moment to stop to see what Fred and Frieda were up to or, more precisely, what latest news they had.

Frieda greeted him cheerfully from behind her counter as he walked into the quiet confines of the town's only drugstore. Frieda was a large, matronly woman in her early sixties and a consistently friendly presence in her establishment. Father John rarely saw either of the Beckers outside their drugstore — Methodists, you know. When they weren't in church it seemed they were most always at work.

The couple never had children but served as surrogate parents for hordes of youngsters who had come into their place of business over the years for fountain treats and quick fixes for a host of minor maladies. The couple was currently dealing with their third generation of such customers. Kids were coming in now whose grandparents had come in decades earlier, and all that time the youthful clientele looked at the Beckers as parental types, that is, people to be trusted and relied on for easy acceptance plus physical nourishment and the ease of soul that came from their reliable presence. And over all those years Fred and Frieda had treated their customers as generously as if they really were their own children, and doing so with hardly a second thought. In any other situation you might expect Frieda to give a kiss or hug to her young clientele. As it was, she unfailingly showered each one with the love that her wide smile and cheerful voice embodied. Father John was the recipient of that as he came in that morning and was immediately cheered by it.

"I know you really want to please me this morning with something that has ice cream in it, but I'll have to think about that, Frieda. It's just nice to get in here for a kind word and a smile. But could you in the meantime please start me off with a Diet Coke. And then come tell me all about what's been happening lately."

He was the only customer and felt sure that Fred would come from the cage at the store's rear to join him and Frieda. He wasn't disappointed. By the time Frieda had brought his drink, Fred was there, and the three began the serious business of the latest town news.

"I must confess I've nothing new for you two," Father John said, "other than a funeral this coming weekend for Maryanne Grimmlesman. She will be shipped in from Tucson for Saturday burial. Remember her?"

"Sure. She moved away, what … three years ago?"

"Your memory's fine, Fred. I'd thought it was maybe four years ago, but when I checked her husband's date of death, it turned out to be a little over three. And she left shortly thereafter. So three years is right on. But that's all the news I have. You two come across anything else?"

"Well, things have been generally hunky-dory lately, but there is one thing. You probably wouldn't know her, but a member of our church, Elsie Hargen, fell and broke her arm," Frieda said. "She was sweeping a critter off her front porch — a cat, I think — and she somehow tripped over the broom. The fall was bad enough, but she tumbled down her three front steps, and that apparently broke her arm.

"As bad as all that was, what made it worse is that she's one of several caregivers to a neighbor of hers, Orville Peckham, another church member. He's housebound and in his upper eighties. Losing her from the rotation of volunteers who help him is putting a strain on the other two ladies, and we're not sure how to replace Elsie ... at least not at this early date. She just broke her arm yesterday. And all this is goin' down as winter's comin' right round the corner. All three volunteers are in Orville's neighborhood, don't you see, and it's easy for them to get over to his place. Now, with someone else, it might not be so easy. The whole church is in a tizzy over this. If you know of anyone who could step in, Father, we'd all be mighty grateful. And you can count on the other two volunteers to break in a new person — you know: give 'em the lowdown on the old man's care.

"There *might* be one or two other church members we could tap for this, but the ones I have in mind are already busy with other things. Removing them from those responsibilities to help Orville is just extending the difficulty because then we'd have to replace *that person* with someone else. You get the picture." She nodded knowingly at the priest.

To Father John it sounded like a needlessly complicated tempest in a teapot, but he didn't dare say that to his friends, sure as he was that Orville's need was real enough. Instead he nodded in shared commiseration and promised to look into some possibilities, though he was quick to add that he could make no promises.

Fred looked at Frieda: "We understand the no-promises part, and we're just very grateful you'll give it a try, Father."

Then Frieda spoke again. "There *is* something else. A rumor's going around that some of the high school kids from Burger are coming over here this Friday night to our Homecoming football game and ramp up the traditional rivalry between the two schools."

"We playing Burger this weekend? I hadn't heard," Father John said.

"No. That's the odd thing. Burger has a free night. For some reason or other they're playing Saturday afternoon … some team from the Chicago area. So if that rumor's true and those kids *are* coming to Algoma, they'll probably be up to no good."

"Are our school officials taking the rumor seriously?"

"They have to, just to play safe. It's going to cost money for extra security. So either way we lose. It'll cost the school district some unbudgeted money, and maybe even we'll end up with trouble anyways, not to mention any cleanup afterward."

"Sounds like I'd better not be out and about Friday night," Father John said. "Have they thought to call the Burger school? Maybe they could head things off?"

"Not a bad idea. Meantime, we don't plan to be out on the street either. In fact, we're closing early and hunkering down at home," Fred said. "I hope nothing comes of this. I don't mind missing the game. Fact is, we attend very few games any more. Climbing bleachers to sit on hard seats is less appealing the older we've gotten. Though, ordinarily I lean toward going to Homecoming."

"Kids," Frieda said. "I love 'em, but every so often … "

Father John nodded sagely but said nothing.

"Oh, I almost forgot," Fred said. "Remember asking about that new family in town, the Dudenbostels? Well, I met the lady of the house last week. She wanted to transfer a prescription from the Burger pharmacy."

"They were using the pharmacy over there?" Father John asked.

"Seems so. But there was some sort of emergency. She ran out of her pills, and we were easier to reach quickly. The doctor who authorized them is back in Ohio somewhere, so they maybe don't have a local one yet. Her name's peculiar, though: Danuta. I even asked her about that, and she said it's Polish."

"Interesting," Father John responded. "I heard they're going to Saints Peter and Paul in Burger. I haven't verified that with Father Jim yet, but I've no reason to disbelieve the report. So they're using the Burger Pharmacy too! Wonder what that's all about. They seem to be boycotting Algoma altogether. But you made a tiny inroad with them. Maybe they'll switch all their prescriptions to you."

"I can only hope so," said Fred, smiling.

The exchange of news apparently at an end, Father John was gone minutes later. But it had been useful. The Dudenbostels had come up again, and little by little their portrait seemed to be emerging.

Homecoming came and went without incident. Perhaps it was just a rumor, Father John thought, although the hastily scheduled Friday night dance at the Burger high school may have helped.

CHAPTER 15

Father John looked at the next few days in his calendar when he returned to the rectory and realized that on the last Sunday night of the month there was a second dinner engagement with friends in Belleville.

In September he had received an invitation to their home for dinner on the last Sunday night of that month and was told that he should stay overnight, as the evening would almost certainly run late.

Monday is technically his day off, though he usually makes little of that. There is no Mass on Monday mornings, so he sometimes sleeps late but rarely leaves Algoma on any jaunt, choosing instead to make home visits and putter around the office, in effect working instead of relaxing. But that particular moment in September proved an exception. He did stay over with his friends and shopped in Belleville the next day, made a stop at the two hospitals to see patients from his county, then shared supper with a priest friend who came in from Smithton. All in all, it had been an enjoyable and relaxing break in his routine, something he should perhaps do oftener.

And the September evening meal with his physician friends had been delightful. They had invited three other couples plus a restaurateur neighbor to that lovely meal. Both of the hosts were internists, and the husband was an accomplished cook. The meal was leisurely, and over coffee at its end, the restaurant owner suggested something that might give them a reason to meet regularly for a few more months.

He proposed that they form two teams and make a bet about a simple card game. The winner of the first game would decide where they would meet the following month and who would host that particular evening, at which time another game would be played and a meal scheduled, and so on until one team had won three games. That would guarantee three or four more months of meal sharing and allow some of the guests to shine as cooks, should they so choose.

They all liked the idea, and after clarifying that the last Sunday night of the month was the ideal time and that the bet be a one-time wager of $25, the matter was settled. The eventual winners would split $250, and Father John was chosen to hold the money.

The game was simple. Five cards would be dealt to each team and the best poker hand would win. As to who should deal, they decided it would be better to spread the whole deck randomly about the table and each person take one card. Then the cards would be laid down one at a time by alternating teams.

So the money was collected and the cards spread. The resulting hand played out dramatically. One couple joined the hosts and Father John to compete against the remaining two couples and restaurant owner, and Father John's team immediately fell behind when the opposing team surfaced an ace, then a queen and a ten. The best Father John's team had come up with was a ten, an eight and a two. But when the other team then turned up a three, Father John turned over a king. They were still behind, but hopeful. The final card for the opposition was a seven, so their hand was still ahead with an ace high. But the evening's hostess turned up a second king, and Father John's team won.

The five winners caucused and named the restaurateur as the next host. But rather than force him to host the event at his restaurant, they left the choice of venue to him. He chose the steakhouse in the casino along the Mississippi in East St. Louis, because he knew the chef and thought he could get a deal. Besides, he said, he knew for certain that the meal would be wonderful.

That's where Father John would be heading on the coming Sunday night. His physician friends told him to stop at their home and they would bring him to the meal. Then he could once again spend the night with them. He was looking forward to another bona fide day off plus one more delightful evening with friends.

And that's indeed what transpired. The restaurant owner brought out a deck of cards for the game at the end of the very delicious steak dinner, but this time the other team won and a third evening was scheduled for late November. Weather permitting, the group would gather at the home of the Carter family in the Signal Hill area of Belleville, a formerly upscale section of town that still enjoyed a reputation as a quiet, somewhat-posh neighborhood. Father John found he was enjoying the group more than he had expected and was looking forward to that third gathering, and again he was to stay over with his medical friends.

But on his Monday evening return to St. Helena's rectory, another clue was waiting for him in the Post-Dispatch box. It said: **THEN WHERE.** It was another teasing message that didn't advance his awareness of the game's final direction! It was maddening, and it dulled the high he felt from the past twenty-four hours.

On Tuesday morning, after seeing the sheriff to give him the new clue, he returned to the courthouse, this time to begin looking at marriage records. He didn't see Pat Kelly, but instead bumped into a retired judge, Hugh Monroe, coming out of the District Attorney's office.

"Your Honor, what brings you here this morning? Have you come out of retirement?"

"No. I just shared a little experience with the DA. He has a case similar to one I presided over some years back. Don't know if it'll help him, but I was glad to get out of the house and consult with him. What brings you here, Father?"

"Oh, I'm looking up some old marriage records. Pretty dull stuff, I expect. But it's good for me to get out of the house too."

"Well, who knows, perhaps we'll have a chance to put our heads together again sometime. The Annie Verden moment was exciting, as I look back on it. Take care, Father." The judge disappeared briskly down the corridor. *He still moves well for an aging man*, Father John thought.

The research did prove to be dull … and fruitless. But Father John had sunk his teeth into the quest to search out the Dudenbostel name and he was not about to give up. When he shut down that day's search, he had gotten to the 1870s. *As elusive as that name is turning out to be, perhaps this is just a silly waste of time. Nonetheless*, Father John decided, *I'll see this out a while longer.*

Halloween came and went before he got back to the courthouse and to his meanderings though the county marriage records. So did All Saints, a holy day he particularly liked. They had sung "For All the Saints" at the Masses and he even chanted the Litany of Saints at the Mass with the largest attendance.

But his next venture at the courthouse proved as pointless as his others. He doubted whether census records would show anything either, because if the family had indeed been in the county at some point, there should have been some birth or death records. Even so, an online plod though census rolls might still be something he would do. He'd have to decide that later.

No clues had shown up for over a week now, and with temperatures in their inevitable November decline, he began to wonder if the game would just peter out. That was the devilish thing about the whole affair. He had been left guessing at every turn but obsessed with it, nonetheless. And he was upset with himself that he had been so easily hooked. Maybe that was the point to this silly game: just rile up the priest!

Most Thursdays the priests of the county met for breakfast after their Masses. Father John didn't often join them, but that second week in November he drove to Germantown for their fellowship. On his way he passed one of the county's oddities: Hillendale Road. There was Crackerneck Road elsewhere in the county and Frogtown, too. Southern Illinois was replete with quaint names that surprised you every so often on jaunts through the countryside.

The priests were in fine form. The bishop never ceased to give them an abundance of things to cluck over, and that morning they were discussing the African priests he had imported over the past few years. Several had actually been called back to Africa recently by their bishops. Originally they had been described as on loan for two or three years, but all had stayed beyond that. And another couple had just arrived.

They were generally good men and all spoke English well, but between their soft-spoken tendencies and accents, most were hard to understand and one or two were unfortunately difficult to get along with. There was also the question of what bringing them here was costing the diocese. It was generally agreed that money had changed hands to bring them here, but no figures were ever shared by the bishop, which still rankled the priests.

There was also a flap about how one of the diocese's priests had been treated by the bishop. Since the new translation of the missal had gone into effect, a priest on the eastern side of the diocese who freely changed the wording of prayers and other parts of the Mass to make the awkward wordings more understandable to his people had been forcibly retired. Then he was suspended from all priestly duties, something most saw as uncalled for and overtly punitive. Since last summer when all that had taken place, a campaign had been mounted and gathered steam in support of the suspended priest. The phenomenon kept the priests abuzz for the greater part of the hour they spent in the restaurant that morning.

Father John had toyed with telling them about his crossword clues, but when he didn't get a good opportunity, he let the matter slide. Afterward he realized that was probably better. None of them were crossword puzzle buffs, and what would they be able to help with, living as they did outside Algoma? Besides, they might speak freely about it and somehow get at cross-purposes with whatever the sheriff was trying to accomplish. But Father John didn't regret the time with his friends that morning. It was refreshing to see their passion for things in the diocese. Such was not always the case, he knew.

Thinking of the sheriff gave him the idea to stop at the jail when he got back into town. Rehashing things couldn't hurt, and perhaps Sheriff Toler had something new.

The lawman seemed surprised but pleased to see the priest and motioned for him to have a seat while he finished a phone call.

When he hung up he asked: "What brings you here? Another clue?"

"No. Just wondering where things stand. You have anything new?"

"No, sorry to say."

"So, no luck with regard to the SUV?"

"Right. I'm beginning to wonder if maybe our perp lives somewhere other than Algoma ... maybe even in St. Louis."

"Or what if that *car* was from outside the town? I mean, perhaps it's only a case of *the car* being from elsewhere."

"You may be onto something. Our search of SUVs in the local area has gotten nowhere. But what if the perp went to the trouble of getting an SUV from far enough away just for that one snowy moment? I hadn't thought of that. Of course, if that *is* the case, I don't know how we can possibly track it, given the little information we have. But I'll keep that in mind. It sure would help if someone had seen something that morning."

"You'd almost think he got lucky with that one moment. How could anyone get such a vehicle on the spur-of-the-moment like that? Of course, he could have recruited a friend to bring one just for that purpose from, as you say, St. Louis."

"More variables to deal with, eh Father?"

"Right. I've asked Horace Denver to keep an eye on things around town. Between him and the young men, who knows what they might get lucky enough to see. But so far, I must admit, none of them have had anything to report. Though, come to think of it, I haven't talked to Horace lately, and I could hunt him down today. In fact, I *will* do that. If I get anything, I'll be sure to let you know. Thanks for your time, Sheriff."

Father John found Horace twenty minutes later, but a short conversation confirmed the priest's suspicions: he hadn't noticed anything worth reporting.

So Father John went home. No new clues there either, no phone messages and no pastorally important things pending. He decided to finalize his next weekend's homily.

CHAPTER 16

Unlike many of his cohorts, Father John wasn't much of a card player. Even so, he went to Burger where on most Sunday evenings the pastor gathered priests for cards — almost always rummy. It might prove to be a good gathering with which to share the crossword clues.

On his way there he drove across the levee where all the trees used to form a canopy over the road. He still hadn't gotten accustomed to their having been cut back so severely. There was no longer a canopy over the road, so in the light of the November moon, it was brightly lit. There were other signs like that of his world changing before his eyes, and in his estimation it was mostly not a good thing.

There was the bishop, who was a growing concern for him and many in the diocese; there were these poor trees on the levee; and there was, of course, the ominous crossword clues. But there were also his body's signs of aging and a growing number of deaths among his friends. He found himself more and more dwelling on such things in his private prayer. Not new phenomena, he realized, in the overall scope of things, but new to him, and when he dwelt on them, more than mildly troubling.

He tried to put such thoughts out of his mind as he drove, refocusing on the highway. It struck him as odd whenever he noticed how far he could drive without having the road as his primary focus. Interesting how the human mind can work!

Some of the same priests who had been at Thursday's breakfast were at the Burger rectory, and the conversation again dwelt on the bishop. Father John made a plea to find something else to talk about, claiming that he was upset enough about *His Excellency*, as the man wished to be called, and didn't need to be reminded how much he was upsetting the diocese. For a while they bantered about other things. Eventually, however, the conversation got back to the bishop, and this time Father John kept quiet.

Given the tenor of their discussion, Father John abandoned all ideas of discussing the crossword clues, and by the end of the evening, though he wasn't ordinarily a very good card player, he returned home with a few more dollars in his pocket and a warmer feeling for his friends in the clergy.

And there were no new clues in his Post-Dispatch box.

Monday morning after sleeping in an extra hour, he arose with an idea floating around in his head about an ad in the Smile. He spent some time thinking that out before going downtown to see Hugh at the paper, but by eleven o'clock he had worked it out sufficiently. When he walked into the newspaper's office, he was feeling rather proud of himself and confident that his idea might work.

What he gave Hugh was a brief text for an ad to be run three times in the weekly paper. The cost was small, but the payoff could be huge, as Father John saw it. The wording was brief and to the point: SEEKING CROSSWORD PUZZLE COLLABORATORS. CONTACT THE SMILE. Hugh was to take all responses and forward them to Father John, who told him that he didn't want to be flooded with responses at the parish. This procedure would insulate him from cranks and he'd be free to weed out those he didn't wish to deal with. The editor didn't seem to mind. Perhaps he thought there wouldn't be that big a response. He agreed to buffer the priest by taking calls and forwarding them. And the deal was done. All Father John had to do now was to sit back and wait for something to come of it.

After leaving the paper, he went to the jail to alert the sheriff. The lawman wasn't in, but his deputy promised to immediately hand over the note Father John had hastily scribbled.

The rest of the day was filled with odds and ends around the rectory: a little reading, several phone calls and a lot of wishful thinking about what he would do if his ad brought results.

CHAPTER 17

Over the next several days, Willy Peters and Tom Bigger stopped at the rectory to tell Father John that they hadn't observed anything that might be of help. The priest thanked them and told them to tell the others about the ad set to appear Thursday in the Smile. If it led to anything, he'd get word to them, probably through Jim Eisner. The sheriff also called to acknowledge that he got word about the ad. He didn't say whether he thought it a good idea.

Father John saw the note on his desk to bring communion to Vera Downing and decided he'd do that Tuesday afternoon. He called to alert her and took off around two. He was surprised to be driving past the Dudenbostel home on his way back from Vera's. He almost stopped when he saw the Honda Harry had mentioned parked in the driveway. He thought for a moment, realized he didn't have a plausible excuse to stop and abandoned the idea. But he'd remember where they lived for another time.

There was a committee of the parish council that dealt with decorative art for the church as well as with special liturgies. While the council itself did not meet in summer, that committee did. In fact, it met monthly because numerous celebrations throughout the year stood in need of their attention.

Several members of that committee had gone to St. Louis that week in November to look at crosses in several churches with a view to perhaps replicating one or more of them for Lenten and Easter ceremonies or even possibly replacing the large cross above the main altar. One of the ladies on the committee had stumbled in the sanctuary of the church and fell, breaking her arm. Father John got the call about her condition just as he returned to the rectory.

She also had a probable concussion from falling onto the marble floor and was in Barnes Hospital. He promised to come immediately, and the committee member told him how and where to park as well as the lady's room number. In little over an hour he was at her bedside.

She was alert and in some pain, but the doctor had assured her that she'd be going home in a day or so, once they were sure about her head trauma. The arm was in a cast and she said *it* didn't hurt. "It's just my head that does, Father. I have a dull headache."

"Well, don't try to talk much or move your head. We'll pray the prayers for the sick with you, and I'll anoint you. When your husband arrives, reassure him that we're besieging heaven for you." He smiled gently at her and gathered the several committee members closer around the bed as he began the comforting liturgy of anointing.

In the waiting area later, he talked with the committee and thanked them for their generosity in spending time on the aesthetics of worship and for coming all the way to St. Louis to do it. They told him it wasn't to have been all work. They had planned to have supper on the Hill after they'd seen the last church. Father John said they should still do so and that he'd join them. In fact, the parish would pay for that meal, and just so Betty wouldn't be left out, they'd send a cannoli or three to the hospital for her and her husband.

At one of the wonderful restaurants on the Hill, as the Italian section of St. Louis is called, they discussed what they had seen and come up with. They were brimming with ideas for Lent and said they particularly liked one of the large crosses they had seen and were, in fact, thinking of recommending its design as a replacement for the large cross above Saint Helena's altar. "If the council likes it, we'll have to find donors to pay for it, of course. But what do you think, Father? Are you open to something like that?"

"I'd like to see what you're proposing, of course, but I'm up for discussing a change. We'd better find out, however, who gave the cross we have now. Don't want to needlessly offend someone. If whoever gave it is still alive or if there are relatives of the donor in the parish, maybe they might even give the new one outright or contribute substantially toward it." Not a bad idea, they all agreed.

The committee members had come in one car, and they said they'd bring the dessert back to the hospital and spend another short visit with Betty. Father John thanked them again, and pointed his Taurus toward Algoma. Several times during the return trip he thanked God for people like that and offered a short prayer that the Lord protect Betty.

CHAPTER 18

The next morning Father John called a committee member to say their report should get to parish council people soon so they'd be prepared to discuss it at the next meeting. The woman told him of a Christmas song she had written. The melody was simple and easy to sing.

It's time again for Christmas,
For all the girls and boys!
For snowy hills and sledding thrills
And angels' joyful noise.

It's time again for Christmas,
And all the world's aglow
With more than toys or shallow joys
Or ribbons in a bow.

O let the whole world hear it:
This is the feast of love.
And peace must reign in hearts worldwide
In grace from God above.

It's time again for Christmas,
And presents by the tree,
For turkey smells and silver bells
With family here near me.

It's time again for Christmas,
May all the lands and seas
Hear loving songs the whole world long
Of quiet, gentle peace.

It's time again for Christmas,
And this must be our prayer:
That every land and every heart
Be blessed with love and care.

Father John liked it and thought it could be sung at Christmas in Saint Helena's, maybe even in Advent. The composer was flattered and said so. She would look forward to its use in church and said she'd get it to the music person soon. Afterward, Father John reflected that there seemed no end to his parishioners' creativity. *Thank goodness they don't rely on me for such things.* Whatever his talents, in his own estimation, artistry and creativity were not among them.

On occasion the campus minister from Southern Illinois University's Newman Center in Carbondale would stop at Saint Helena's for confession. Father Ed Wallen's parents lived nearby, and confession to Father John was very convenient. Many times they then spent time in conversation afterward. Ed Wallen showed up at Saint Helena's just before noon, and when the confession was finished, Father John suggested they go to the truck stop for lunch.

Over the blue plate special, the two got to discussing a book the Newman chaplain had read recently. Father John listened intently to the younger man's monologue. The book was Daniel Kahnerman's Thinking, Fast and Slow and dealt with the way humans think. As he tried to absorb what the younger man was saying, Father John realized several things: this was not a book he'd have ordinarily heard about or be attracted to; it was precisely the kind of fare he'd expect someone at a university to pick up on; and despite all that, he found what the young priest was saying to be surprisingly interesting.

The author was an Israeli psychologist who had won a Nobel Prize in economics. The research for the book came out of his trying to assess leadership skills among army recruits. The author quickly discovered that the predictive results his team developed were often faulty, in part because team members were often reluctant to change methods despite evidence that what they were doing wasn't working.

He said he got lucky in meeting a fellow Israeli academic named Taversky who was trained in mathematics and decision theory, and he came to realize the large role that luck and chance play in how we process decisions and review experiences. He worked with this professor to uncover all sorts of irrational biases, cognitive illusions and systematic errors that are built into human thinking, even in that of highly trained or otherwise very bright people.

Father John interrupted. "This is fascinating. What does it mean about our attempts as Christians, especially so-called professional Christians like you and me, to evangelize others?"

"A very good question, one I've been pondering in my work among college students at SIU. I'm not sure, John, about that, but it's got me thinking a lot lately. And I figured you might be interested as well. I know how pastoral you are ... " Father John blushed slightly. "So far all I've come up with is that the role of the Spirit must be huge any time we're said to succeed in overtly passing on the faith.

"Kahnerman identifies two kinds of thinking. What he calls System I is a kind of built-in result of eons of evolution that works fast and effortlessly in an intuitional way and takes for granted that what we see or experience is all there is. And it jumps to conclusions based on that background and the data from many experiences.

"System II is the rational, logical, calculating kind of thought that seeks to control System I, but it's lazy about it, often allowing biases, illusions and errors to slip past. It's as though the slow and deliberate effort to make corrections is easily abandoned because it's too much work. The result is often that errors are endorsed and become the conscious beliefs, attitudes and intentions that are then routinely and regularly applied to even important things in life.

"Take, for example, our political scene. That's one good example of what can result from this. Another is the reality behind never arguing politics or religion. Kahnerman says we're well-trained or -developed to be intuitional thinkers, and we find it hard to do the slow and calculated work of challenging a plausible-sounding story that System I thinking might present to us. If something sounds familiar or fits our experiences or habits, we often accept it easily and, in effect, resist anyone or anything that might try to contradict it.

"You and I, as well as others in professional fields, have had some training in systematic thought and/or academic areas that involve research. We know how slow and plodding the work of establishing or proving a theory can be. We know that what people who come us want are quick, black-and-white and simple answers. And we well recognize that usually the matters in question are complicated, not capable of being explained easily or quickly, and gray, rather than black and white.

"But the fascinating thing to me is that Kahnerman notes that *even we* act like those people. For all our training, we also easily accept biases, errors and the like and find distasteful any clunking through the hard work to investigate and perhaps disprove something we hold near the level of absolute truth. Isn't that fascinating?"

"As I think about it, I believe you're right. What's to be done, then, Ed? It sounds like a dilemma."

"As I understand him, Kahnerman says we should appreciate the value of System I thought because it's essential to surviving and to living creatively and pleasurably. But because it's prone to leaving us with biases and errors, we need to slow down and use the logical thought of System II to check things out when the stakes are high. That kind of balance is necessary and implies that we need be ready to check ourselves. His book tries to give us some tools for that.

"So our training's strong emphasis on rationality isn't so far off base, after all. We may teach moral behavior best by modeling it, but the rational background, the logical way we pick it apart and try to understand it, is the right *underpinning* after all. And we shouldn't abandon it. We just need to realize that it may not work its magic on someone quickly or instantly. And I think we were led to believe while we were in our schooling that it ought to."

"You've given me a lot to mull over, but I'm going to try. I'm really glad you stopped today, Ed. Maybe we can revisit this again sometime."

Father John's mind was awhirl as he parted from his young friend. But he found his mental tornado exciting.

CHAPTER 19

Father John returned from the truck stop to find a message awaiting him on his answering machine. Olivia Lanner had died just minutes ago. Bobbie Sue had called from the bank to tell him about the death of the bank president's wife. The two were Methodists, but Bobbie Sue knew that Mr. Lanner and Father John were on a first name basis and that he would want the priest to know about his wife's death.

Father John immediately called Bob Lanner's private secretary. There had been a massive heart attack and Olivia was dead before the EMTs arrived. Father John thanked Bobbie Sue for her thoughtfulness and promised to be of help in whatever way he could. And she promised to relay that to her boss.

He put the phone down and reflected on the fact that he had been to the Lanner house only once. That mansion was one of the four or five old-money houses on *the* big hill in Algoma and within a block of Annie Verden's house and the Murdoch place. Nowadays the occupants of those old and elegant homes, with the exception of Bob Lanner, were no longer the ultra-rich of the town, but the houses nonetheless looked magnificent and were well maintained.

The occasion that had found him inside the Lanner mansion was a small celebration at the completion of a local fund drive several years earlier. Money had been raised for the planting of trees in the park and on Main Street, and Bob Lanner as committee chairman had overseen that campaign. Father John was on the committee and with other members attended the exclusive dinner party hosted by a beaming Robert and Olivia Lanner.

It was not only the one time he saw the inside of their home, it was the only time he ever met Olivia, Bob's second wife. He had remarried four years after the death of his first wife, much to the surprise of his friends. He was well into his sixties at the time, and Olivia was barely forty, for one thing. For another, she was not originally from Algoma and a Baptist to boot. But she graciously switched her religious allegiance to the Methodist Church and from all accounts made a charming and comforting wife for the banker. That being said, she was not often seen outside their gorgeous old home because Bob was no longer in the habit of making many public appearances. He was at the bank every working day and regularly attended the Algoma Methodist Church. But beyond that, he mostly kept to himself in his mansion, enjoying married life quietly according to all reports. He did appear at the occasional backyard barbecues Bobbie Sue and her husband hosted, but Olivia never came with him, and he never stayed long.

What Father John remembered of the elegant old home was its high ceilings, Victorian bric-a-brac in almost every room, the pocket doors between the dining and living rooms — perhaps the latter was called the parlor — and the servants' stairs off the kitchen leading to the four bedrooms upstairs. Annie Verden's home had a similar back stairs, he recalled.

At the front of the house was a beautiful curved stairway to the second floor, the start of which stairway was just inside the huge front door in an otherwise spacious lobby. Dominating that front lobby was a massive grandfather clock whose bell tones were deep and sonorous. Father John heard them ringing every fifteen minutes throughout that evening of the party, but the chiming pattern was one he did not recognize, surely not the usual Westminster chimes most such clocks used.

Father John debated with himself for several minutes about driving to the banker's home to offer his personal condolences then thought better of the idea. There would be time enough for that the night of the wake at Feldspar's. But he was certain that the loss would hit the banker terribly hard.

The next day he was surprised by a call from Feldspar's asking that, at Mr. Lanner's request, he be a part of the service at the cemetery. He immediately agreed but was determined to get more details from Bob Lanner at the wake. He didn't understand exactly what he was to do: simply be present, offer a prayer or a eulogy, or conduct the entire burial service. In any event, he felt honored to be asked.

At the next evening's wake, Bob Lanner told him in hushed tones: "I'm sure you know why I've asked you to conduct the burial service at the cemetery, and it's all right with our minister. Allow him to offer a prayer though, and please don't eulogize Olivia. That will be done at church. And I'm hoping you can attend that service too, Father.

"You probably had no way of knowing, but Olivia liked you ever since that evening at our home some years ago. I'm sorry she

86

didn't have a chance to tell you so. I'll miss her … " His voice trailed off and he looked for a moment as though he would break into tears. But he shook Father John's hand and quickly turned to the next person waiting to offer condolences.

Father John couldn't help but think back to when he and the banker had talked extensively about Annie Verden and Horace Denver, and he only now realized how close it had drawn them. He would be glad to preside at Olivia's burial the next morning.

After the funeral at the Methodist church, Father John found himself alone again in the hearse with Lawrence Feldspar. His trip to the cemetery earlier in the fall had been pleasant, but it turned out to be somewhat less exciting than most trips with Larry Sr. This time, however, the old man was back in form. He told two brief but funny stories about Protestant ministers at funerals his firm had conducted. Father John had to compose himself before stepping out of the hearse at the cemetery.

The service went well, and Bob Lanner told him again how grateful he was for being a part of it. When the priest was back in the hearse with Mr. Feldspar, he asked him to not return immediately so he could ask a question or two about a monument he had seen near Olivia's gravesite.

"Do you know anything about that very large tombstone just to the east of Olivia's grave? Is it on the city side of the cemetery or is it in our Catholic cemetery?"

"It's at the edge of the city cemetery, but I'm not sure which side of the line it's actually on."

"Whose is it … or *what* is it?"

"I'm 99% sure it's a tombstone, but I don't know whose it is. It is, if I remember correctly, the largest monument in either cemetery. Eons ago — well before my time — the city set a limit on the height of grave markers and that one, I guess, came in just under the wire. Why do you ask about it?"

"Well, for one thing, if it's in our cemetery, I should know more about it. Anyway, it's a curiosity, for sure, and I just want to know what I can about it. It's the first time I noticed it."

"I'm sure I can find out if it's that important, Father. Want me to?"

"If you don't mind. Give me a call when you know more. And there's certainly no rush."

"I've plenty of time. I should be able to get on it today … tomorrow, for sure. But sometime you must ask me about the old Packard hearse we have in the garage back at the funeral home. It's a Henney from the '30s, so it's probably older than you or me, Father. I'll show it to you sometime. I might even take you for a spin in it."

"So long as you don't make me ride in back, Larry," he said and smiled as he prepared to get out. He thanked him as they were pulling up to his place, promised to come to see that antique and, with a wave, got out and headed into Saint Helena's rectory.

CHAPTER 20

The next day Larry Feldspar called just after morning Mass.

"I found out a lot about that tombstone, Father. It's just inside the boundary line between the cemeteries on your side of the line. It was put there by a family named Polovitski and is unique in that there are grave plots on each of the four sides of the monument. However, it seems that there's only one body buried there. The other three plots are empty, according to the courthouse records. We didn't have that funeral because it was before my father opened up shop here in town."

"Do you know the name of the person buried there, Larry?" Father John asked. "With any luck what you've found will jibe with my records. And when was that burial? I suppose it was the same time that the large grave marker was erected."

"Suppose so. The burial was in 1889, and the deceased was a Danuta Polovitski, wife of Anton."

"I never knew there had been Poles in our parish, and that was so long ago that I imagine no one here has any memory of that family. Maybe the oldest of our records has something about them. Thanks, Larry. That was beyond the call of duty. I owe you."

The funeral director laughed and hung up.

The gravestone was unique in several ways, Father John realized. He wanted to go back for a closer look, but from what he remembered, it was very tall and had a pyramidal shape rising from above the large square base. Perhaps there were crosses on that lower square segment, but there wasn't one atop the structure. The pyramid simply tapered to a point at the top and ended there, looking like a needle sticking up. Strange for a Catholic grave marker!

He got to the cemetery the next day. A chilly November wind was blowing, and Father John had to walk a good bit to the gravesite from where he could park. Two names were etched into the stone. Danuta Polivitski, born in 1851, died in 1899, the wife of Anton. The other was Anton Polivitski, and only his birth date was indicated: July 9, 1848. There were crosses alongside both names, but none atop the monument, and the other two sides were blank.

Father John had found the name in the parish burial records and learned that thee were two children, both baptized at Saint Helena's: Anton, Jr. and Emilia. The records had nothing more: when and or how they came to America, where they lived in Algoma, when they moved away, nothing. But Danuta's burial record had a curious addition: *buried with balalaika.* Father John had to look that up and was surprised to find it was something like a guitar, popular mostly in Russia. Perhaps the family had come from the eastern side of Poland and got the instrument there. He could only imagine them bringing it all the way across the ocean to the new world. And which of them played it? Probably the wife.

He also wondered about the name Danuta. It was the second time he had heard it. He found out that it means Danielle or Donna and is popular among Polish women. *So it's a common name.* He had dealt with very few Poles and was unfamiliar with it.

But the fact that the stone topped out to a point perplexed him. *Is there something especially Polish about that? Poland's very*

Catholic. You'd think the stone would have a cross on top. But he couldn't puzzle it out any further and finally put the matter out of his mind once his original curiosity had been satisfied.

But by that time he had worked on it a good part of the day, so he decided to buy a sandwich in town for supper. As he left his driveway, he spotted another clue in his paper box. It read: ***VERY NEAR***. *Another one delivered in daylight hours!*

So the clues thus far now read: ***Intrigued you should be you are it I'm coming for you but when not yet they're cross words soon then where very near.*** The ominous message had become very scary. It looked more and more to Father John like someone was out to get him, maybe even at Saint Helena's. But he still had no idea why he should be some sadistic or deranged person's target.

Instead of getting a sandwich, he went straight to the sheriff, taking care to handle the clue with his handkerchief again. The deputy had to call the sheriff at home, and the lawman came right over.

"The message is starting to make sense, but I don't like it."

"*You* don't like it! *I'm* getting very worried. Up 'til now it might've been just a game. Now I'm not so sure," Father John said.

The two chatted awhile, but little else was decided. The sheriff spoke about possible police protection. Father John wasn't sure how that would work and said his first reaction wasn't a favorable one. But the two agreed to think it over and talk more soon.

The sandwich Father John finally got wasn't as satisfying as he had hoped. And he didn't sleep well that night, either.

CHAPTER 21

On Monday, a day he could have been enjoying as a day off, Father John instead went to the Catholic hospital in Burger to visit the one parishioner he knew was there. But as he often did, he looked at the roster of Catholic patients to see if he knew any of them and was surprised to see the name Dudenbostel.

Herman Dudenbostel had been admitted over the weekend and was on a floor that indicated a non-life-threatening condition. There were two other patients from elsewhere in the county and Father John went to see them first, saving Herr Dudenbostel for last, in case the conversation got lengthy. *Herman, eh? Couldn't sound more German!*

When he walked into the Dudenbostel room fifteen minutes later, he was surprised to see it was a private room, perhaps reflecting the money his highly placed position at Scott Field guaranteed him ... that information according to the young men who first reported his presence in Algoma. *Good! That'll allow us to converse freely.*

"Hello, Mr. Dudenbostel. You don't know me, I suppose. I'm Father John Wintermann, pastor of Saint Helena's in Algoma. I'm here to see a parishioner and decided to look in on you as well because you're also from Algoma. What brings you in here, if I may ask?"

"Thanks for stopping, Father. My diabetes acted up, and they're trying to adjust my insulin dosage. I guess I fudged too much in the past few weeks. My wife loves to bake and I got carried away with the pie she made. They've got me on a pretty strict diet here, and the blood sugar has dropped a lot. Even so, they're still not satisfied they've got my insulin intake right, so I'll probably be here another day, maybe two."

"I'd heard your family recently arrived in town but I wasn't sure if you are Catholic. I see on the hospital list, however, that you are."

"We're attending church here in Burger, Father. My wife wanted to do that, and it made no difference to me."

"Someone thought your family was originally from this county, perhaps even from Algoma. Is that so?"

"No, we Dudenbostels were never from around here. My ancestors came over in the 1830s from the northern part of Germany through New Orleans. They then went up the Mississippi all the way to the Twin Cities where they quickly moved out into farming areas in the Dakotas. My forebears were originally farmers near Hamburg.

"They stayed around the Dakotas — mostly near Fargo — for a generation or two before my father got a job in Milwaukee. That lasted barely two years, then he landed a much better one in Chicago, and we lived there when I was a boy. The North Side ... Saint Cornelius parish, actually. Know where that is?" Father John shook his head.

"I met my wife there. She lived in the Lincoln Square area and went to Transfiguration. She's from a Polish family, whose immigration story is totally different from mine, as you might guess. Anyway ... Is this boring you? I've been running on and on, something I tend to do."

"Quite the contrary. Just keep on *running on*," Father John said with a smile.

"Well, as I started to say, I joined the Air Force a good while after the Korean War and was able to get a good education. And the Air Force experience eventually helped me land a civilian job with that branch of service. I moved up the ladder and recently ended up at Scott Field.

"We liked what we'd learned about Algoma and the county here. It's near enough to Scott, so we decided to put down roots here ... for at least a while. You never know with government jobs! But this one looks like I might be able to hold onto it for quite a while, maybe even retire from it. At that point we'll probably head back to Chicago. Lots of time to change our minds several times, even."

"Your family must take your German heritage seriously."

"Why do you say that? Because we moved to a place where lots of Germans have settled?"

"I was thinking more about your first name. Herman isn't one that even the residents here use much any more."

The patient laughed as he wiggled around to sit up a bit straighter in bed. "That's certainly been true of the generations before me here in the United States, including my father's. But with my generation there's less commitment to that. I suppose it also reflects that fact that my elders mostly married Germans, while my generation hasn't. I married a Pole, and my brother and sister married Italians. Other cousins did similarly. All three of us in my family also moved

94

away from family enclaves. But, yes, Herman certainly makes me easy to identify in an ethnic crowd … or any group, I guess."

"Your wife's Polish? Are her roots strongly so or is she, like you, part of a generation that's been assimilated? You know, our famous melting pot."

"*Sort of*, I'd say. We tend to spend more time with her family than with mine, but our children don't have either Polish or German names. Jerry is named for an uncle on her side and Mary for an aunt on mine. They're both out of college and married, and they live as far away as they could be, one on the East Coast and the other on the West Coast. But I suppose you *could* say that my wife still has an interest in her Polish heritage … more than I do in mine, for sure. She's putting together a family tree and wants me to do one for my side of the family. She even promised to help me, so I suppose I'll eventually have to get involved with that."

"Have you had diabetes long?"

"It came to light four or five years ago. I found out it's in my family too. Not my father's generation, but the one above it. I'm told the genetics often involve skipping a generation, though at my doctor's advice I've warned my kids to be alert for signs of it in themselves and their children. There's only one grandchild so far, and he's not yet two. So far, nothing's shown up with my kids or Ethan, my grandson. That's certainly not a German name either, is it?

"You know, I'm pretty proud of my kids. Even though my daughter lives on the left coast …"

Father John cut in: "*Left* coast?"

"Yeah. You know: all the left-wingers out there, especially in California. She doesn't live *there*, though. She's up in Seattle because her husband works for Boeing. But despite being there, she's still a Republican, I'm happy to say. Although she *has* changed *some* … gotten much more interested in ecological stuff, which is good, I suppose. She and her husband both bicycle whenever they can, and they're big into recycling. And she's still very Catholic. They attend at the cathedral in Seattle and when we went out there to visit recently, she introduced my wife and me to a service called Taize. Ever hear of it?" Father John nodded. "I liked it a lot, very meditative and spiritual.

"And my son lives in Massachusetts — Boston — he also goes to church regularly. But, sad to say, I think he's become a Democrat, probably thanks to his wife. He hasn't said so exactly and it's not something easily brought up and best left unsaid, but Dannie and I think he has … from some things he says.

"But we love them both, our kids, and we see them a couple of times a year. We can hop military flights, and that helps a lot. We figure we're better off with our kids than a whole lot of other parents we know, especially those in the service."

"Thanks for sharing all that about your family, Herman. But I don't want to tire you out with my prattle or questions," Father John said. "If you and your wife want to switch to Saint Helena's I … we … will be happy to welcome you. What's her name, by the way? I don't think I got it." Father John knew, of course but didn't want Herman to know that.

"Danuta. But I call her Dannie."

96

"Oh, that's the Danny you mentioned moments ago. But that's a boy's name. Can you use it for a woman too?"

"D A N N I E," he spelled, and smiled. "You're not the only one who's been confused about that. It's a nickname for Danielle. Some Polish women here in the States prefer *Donna*. My Danuta likes *Dannie*."

"Thanks again for the conversation, Herman. I hope they get the blood sugar thing figured out quickly so you can go home."

Father John realized on his way back home that he had a lot to process when he got there.

CHAPTER 22

Thanksgiving was still several weeks away and the weather was getting chillier by the day. On Wednesday the first frost showed up, though the temperature was back up into the low 40s by noon.

Father John had spent a day and a half thinking about the Dudenbostels between ministerial duties. It proved something of a relief from preoccupation with the crossword clues. That they were Republicans was no big surprise. Many southern Illinoisans were, as were numerous people in the armed services, though their coming from Chicago might have aligned them otherwise. That they were staunch Catholics wasn't surprising either. But their not attending church in Algoma where they lived was puzzling. *Why was that again? The wife's decision and easily acceptable to him? What was that all about? Was Herman a wimp? Didn't seem so. Why would she want that?*

Father John couldn't wrap his mind around that. The puzzlement about it continued to bother him: good Catholics, but not wanting to attend Mass here! Why go elsewhere? There had to be a reason, but he couldn't figure what it could be.

Late Wednesday morning something finally got his mind onto other things. Conrad Eversman called him with an invitation. "Julia and I would like you to join us tonight. We're going to Tony's in Mascoutah, and it's been so long since we've visited with you that it's a no-brainer to invite you along. Can you come?"

"How nice of you! I'd love to, Coonie. What time should we hook up? And do you want me to drive?"

"Oh, no. We've got a new Lincoln from the dealership. Our sons keep us well-wheeled," Coonie said, "and I'm sure it's more comfortable than your old Taurus. We'll pick you up around five, if that's okay."

"Five works for me. Thanks, again. I haven't been to Tony's in a long time, either."

"And speaking of your Taurus, Father, I'm sure I can convince my sons to give you a good deal if you want something newer."

"You're still a salesman, Coonie, even in retirement. We can talk on the way about that, but I probably won't be in the market for anything just yet. My car doesn't even have 100,000 miles on it yet and still purrs like a pussycat. See you tonight."

The conversation was light on the way to the restaurant. Julia and Conrad were enjoying good health; the dealership was surviving the recession, and the families of both sons were doing well. When Father John brought up the new family in town, Julia remarked that they'd been around for some months already, so they weren't *that* new. Father John acknowledged that and asked if either of his friends knew them.

Julia did. "Dannie and I are involved in the Women's Garden Club and we've already headed up several recycling campaigns on the west end of the county. She's very committed to environmental stuff."

"What's that mean, Jules? I mean, what's involved in that?"

"Oh, we've spoken at three high schools and several elementary schools ... about the value to the planet when we re-use resources like paper. It's been fun, and we've gotten good at it."

"What's she like as a person?" Father John asked.

"Sweet. And very Catholic, I've discovered."

"But they don't attend Saint Helena's. Did you know that?"

"No, I didn't. I just figured they went on Sunday, since Coonie and I most always go Saturday evenings. I'm surprised. Wonder why they don't go here?"

"Me too, although I met her husband the other day at the hospital. He was in for some adjustment to his meds. I didn't ask why they're going to Burger, but before I could even bring it up, he said his wife wanted to and he went along with it. He seems nice ... pretty talkative. I learned that their two kids are married and live one on each coast. He works at Scott, and they can get military flights to visit them, he told me."

"You learned more about their family than I have. But I do know she's Polish ... and he's German ... obviously ... with a name like that. But you probably knew that already, I'm guessing," Julia said.

"Only just learned it the other day. A young man who told me they'd recently moved here thought the Dudenbostels had a history in town, but Herman says otherwise. He and his wife are Chicagoans, though like many folks, their ancestors lived in a number of places after immigrating here. It's puzzling why they don't come to Saint Helena's. If you hear anything about that, Jules, let me know. I hope it's not something I said or did that has turned them off ... or *her*, because she's the one behind their going to Burger, as I said."

With that they arrived at the restaurant, where they had steaks — Coonie and Julia shared one — and healthy salads from the salad bar. The three shared one piece of pie afterward, deciding to forego the ice cream with it. Then they lingered over coffee and spoke with the restaurant's owner. Coonie sold him a couple of cars in the old days, and when he spotted him in the restaurant, he called him over to chat.

On the way home, Father John brought them up to speed on Maryanne Grimmlesman's funeral, and Coonie and Julia reminisced about their connections to her over the years. When at last the couple dropped him back at the rectory, Father John thanked his old friends for a delightful evening. Going inside by way of the front door, he didn't even think to check his paper box by the back door for a new clue.

CHAPTER 23

On Thursday morning, however, there was nothing new in the paper box, and Father John thought he'd check his traps. The five young men had nothing new to offer; Pat Kelly didn't, either; the ad in the Smile had gone nowhere; and Horace Denver had nothing. The sheriff told him he was at a dead end on the SUV, and when Father John hung up from the final phone call to the jail just before lunch, he felt depressed. The matter had gone on for months, and he was no closer to a solution than ever.

He had already told the sheriff that he wanted nothing to do with police protection, although without telling Father John, the lawman had begun sending patrol cars past the rectory more often. But on Friday morning another clue showed up outside the rectory: *AND WHY*. And the sheriff's patrol cars hadn't seen anyone place it there.

There was still no clarification to the emerging message … just more teasing and suspense by prolonging things! *Whoever's doing this has certainly got my attention.*

The following Monday morning he received a call from Tim O'Brien, the pastor of Saint Joseph's in Benton. "I'm getting cabin fever down here, John, and I want to come up your way to do some hunting."

"I didn't know you were an outdoorsman, Tim. Can't you do that sort of thing down your way?"

"No, not that kind of hunting, John. Not with a *gun* … with a *camera*. I want to take some pictures of autumnal flora and fauna and maybe get some shots over at Carlyle Lake. I'm thinking of putting together a book about death and dying."

"Sounds interesting. When do you want to come?"

"I could come tomorrow or Wednesday, and I hope to stay over with you one night before coming back to Benton."

"You pick the day. Either works for me," Father John said.

"Then I'll come tomorrow. Should be at your place by noon."

"Good. We'll have lunch and then you can go on safari."

"I had in mind that you'd go with me. We can talk over lunch."

Father John knew Tim as one of the creative and interesting younger priests in the diocese. He was not yet fifty and was one of the few artsy-craftsy guys in the presbyterate. A good liturgist and preacher, he was much loved in the little parish in Benton, and while the two priests didn't often get together, whenever they did, Father John always had a good time. You never knew what the younger man might be up to or into. *This time it's photography … and what else did he say? A book he was putting together … about death and dying. I'll have to have a long conversation with him to find out what that's all about.*

Lunch provided new clues to what Tim had in mind. Father John was to drive him to numerous places but wouldn't necessarily have to tromp around in the wild as Tim searched for photo ops. But that meant Father John would spend as much as a day and a half with

Tim, mostly waiting in his car for Tim to finish getting just the right images. He'd bring something to read.

That process began just after lunch that very day and went on until dark. In the evening Tim showed Father John the digital images he had captured, plus a poem he intended to put into the book.

HOW IS IT THAT NOW ALL THIS LONG

SO MANY THINGS HAVE SLIPPED AWAY — STEALTHILY, AT BEST:

MOURNED AND GRIEVED, GONE AT NO PARTICULAR BEHEST —

RUN AFOUL OF WHAT, I WONDER — AND NO SIGNS OF IT ALL ALONG,

BUT BUSINESS, ROUTINE AS USUAL?

WHEN DID I BEGIN TO WOBBLE, WHEEZE AND MOVE SO SLOW,

COMMENCE TO DODDER, CREEP AND FIND IT HARD TO STAY ASLEEP?

OTHERS GOT OLD. DID I AS WELL? AND WAS IT ONE GREAT LEAP?

OR WAS IT PIECEMEAL, TO DELAY MY COMING TO KNOW?

IT ALL LEAVES ME FEELING QUITE ... UNUSUAL.

IT'S NOT THE WRINKLES OR LACK OF BREATH

NOR DIZZINESS WHEN RISING FROM A CHAIR —

BUT RATHER THOSE LOOKS, THE PATRONIZING STARES

AND KNOW-IT-ALL SYMPATHY FROM THOSE STILL FAR FROM DEATH —

PLUS MY KNOWING THEY ARE RIGHT, HOWEVER SHORTSIGHTED.

THEY TOO WILL FOLLOW. SHOULD THAT NOT CAUSE THEM PAUSE?

AND WHETHER OR NO, WHY IS THIS EITHER WAY

NO CONSOLATION TO ME, NO EXECUTION'S STAY?

BOUND ARE WE ALL BY SUCH INEXORABLE AND NATURAL LAWS,

I KNOW. BUT WHY ARE WE — YES, WE ALL — SO BENIGHTED?

Tim was pretty much a Renaissance man. The only human endeavor he wasn't into was athletics. He played piano and one other instrument — Father John could never remember which one. He told Father John once that he had taken up painting: watercolors, and it was obvious from talking with him that he was well-read; and he was a good cook to boot — one of only a very few priests of the diocese who bothered.

"Where'd you find that poem, Tim?"

"I wrote it. Like it?"

And now here was some poetry of his! Always surprises with Tim! "I do like it. So then, this whole book of yours will sound like that poem?"

"No, only in part. Along with the images of autumn — you know, the stark landscapes, the black-and-white textures, the barren trees, the animals and birds in winter coats and plumage — I also want some text that speaks of hope and the proper balance of beginnings and endings as part of the overall grand cycle of life. Americans tend to not see death as part of life and its culmination,

105

something to be celebrated rather than feared. It should be viewed as one thing in a great cycle of life as God intended it to be. So the poem will be a part of that, not the whole of it by any means, and certainly not the high point.

"But the rest of the text is proving tricky. I'd like to put a story in about an Amish farmer who notices a man drinking from his pond with his hand. The Amish man shouts: 'Trinken Sie nicht das Wasser, die Kuhe und die Schweine haben darin geschiessen!' (Don't drink the water. The cows and the pigs have gone in it!) The man shouts back: 'I'm an American Muslim, I don't understand your gibberish. Speak English, infidel!' The farmer shouts back: "Use both hands. You'll get more!"'"

Father John snickered. "Funny. But what's it got to do with death?"

"You could die from drinking infected water."

"That's too much of a stretch, Tim. I don't think you should use it. Besides, it's racist and maybe also mean."

"You're right, I'm sure. But some John Denver lyrics might work. In Rhymes and Reasons he sings: 'So you speak to me of sadness and the coming of the winter ... we must begin to seek the wisdom of the children and the graceful way of flowers in the wind. For the children and the flowers are my sisters and my brothers. Their laughter and their loveliness could clear a cloudy day. Like the music of the mountains and the colors of the rainbow, they're a promise of the future and a blessing for today.' That's too long, but some of it could be just right for the book. I've got to find a way to weave it in."

'I hope you can pull that off. The words are lovely and fit what you're trying to say. Your book sounds pretty ambitious, but if anyone can pull it off, I believe you can, young man."

"A lot of the text is finished. I especially need the right images now, and I figured I could find some stuff here that I can't get down around Benton or in the Shawnee Forest. Today's outing confirmed that. I'll go out alone tomorrow, and if I finish in time, I'll call so we can do lunch. Otherwise you won't hear from me. Either way I'll drive home in the afternoon. What time's Mass tomorrow? I'll concelebrate, if that's okay."

"Sure. Eight o'clock. Want to preach a short homily?"

"Glad to. Breakfast later at the truck stop?"

As he went to bed, Father John toyed briefly with letting Tim in on the crossword stuff.

CHAPTER 24

Tim's homily was superb. And having thought about it overnight, Father John decided to bring him on board about the crossword clues. He lived far enough away that he wouldn't alert anyone in Algoma should he mention something. Over battercakes, bacon and coffee at the truck stop he swore him to secrecy nonetheless and gave him the whole story, beginning with the crossword idea that was floated to the Post-Dispatch all the way through to the latest clue in his rectory's paper box.

Tim listened with eager fascination. When Father John finished, he said: "I don't want to seem callous about your worries, John. They're genuine enough, all right, I'm sure. But I hope you'll pardon me for saying this sounds exciting. I'm sure you're right to bring the sheriff in on this, but it's possible that you've both missed a few angles about how to approach the matter. Think outside the box with me for a moment here.

"What do you think is the significance of the phone call you got calling them *crosswords*? And, by the way, was that one word or two as best you could tell from the person's voice?"

"I'm pretty sure it was two, Tim. The caller enunciated very slowly and carefully, pausing between the words. So I think it was meant to be two words, not one. Why?"

"Well, then I think we need to figure out as many meanings for the word *cross* as we can.

"First off, and most obviously, it could simply mean cross as in crosswords. You've pretty much been locked into that already, I believe. But it could also mean a host of other things: cross as in angry. What might someone have to be angry about?

"Or cross as in to *cross over* something or cross from one thing or place to another. You know, transition. What might that refer to?

"Or maybe it's cross as in cruciform. What shapes like that could he or she be referring to … some landmark around here, maybe? Isn't there a plague cross in the county?"

Father John nodded.

"Or what if it's a religious reference? Some cross in or above a church. Or maybe the cross of Jesus. Or a cross on a tomb or rosary? Or one on a wall in a home, a church, a public building.

"Or what if you're supposed to hook up those clues into a bunch of little crosses … or one big one? That would be clever! Have you tried that already?"

Father John shook his head. "I have to admit, I've ignored almost all those possibilities, and so has the sheriff, Tim … not even thought about them, actually."

After taking a breath, Tim continued as though he were unstoppable. "You know, it could be a symbol printed somewhere in a more or less famous publication, or etched on a building or a monument. There's also the really weird possibility that it's more than one of the above. I mean, this person does seem to want to lead you on, perhaps confuse you, so it *could be* some weird combination of things.

"Although ... the words *I'm coming for you* were used, right? That's pretty obviously ominous. But that could mean I'm coming for you *by or alongside some cruciform thing or other*, or I'm coming for you *because of* some cruciform thing or other." He finally slowed to a stop and stared into space for a moment as though double-checking some mental list.

Then he looked back at the older priest. "I know I've hit you with a whole lot of stuff all at once, and it might not seem helpful right off the bat. But the idea is to get you thinking about various possibilities in case one of them sparks an idea in your head. You've got some thinking to do about all this stuff.

"Is that helpful ... at least some of it? Or did I just complicate your thoughts so much that they're now a muddled mess?"

"Well, nothing has jumped out at me yet, so I guess it *is* a bit muddled right now. But I think — I hope — it's going to be helpful in the long haul. I'll run these things past the sheriff and perhaps a couple of the other people I've let in on this — the more minds the better for this kind of brainstorming, I figure — and we'll see what develops.

"Also, the more I think about that kind of process, the more hopeful I feel. In fact, this has restored some energy in me. I have to admit that I've recently been feeling down because of no light at the end of my tunnel. But you've given me some new directions, new possibilities for unearthing a reason behind this crazy, sadistic game someone's running on me. Thanks, Tim. Breakfast is on me. And good luck with your book."

Father John couldn't wait to talk with Sheriff Toler, and if the lawman would agree, he planned to do the same with the young men and perhaps Pat Kelly. Maybe, just maybe, they were getting somewhere.

When he got home from the jail later, he felt a small celebration was in order. He had to root around in his closet for a bottle because he really didn't drink that much, but he eventually found an almost full bottle of bourbon. He poured a little into a glass, added some water and sat in his favorite chair, nursing the drink and ruminating over what Tim had said ... and welcoming back some feelings of hope.

CHAPTER 25

Father John sat for a long time mulling over what Tim had said and by early afternoon, when no call had come in from the Newman chaplain, he grabbed a quick ham sandwich and placed a call to Rick Binz asking him to check with the others about coming to the rectory the next evening. Then he called Pat Kelly with the same request. By suppertime he had confirmations from all but Tom Bigger, who begged off because of a family commitment but promised to get brought up to speed about anything that came out of the gathering.

The next evening when his confidants were seated in his living room, Father John relayed what Father Tim O'Brien had given him to think about. Then he reviewed the clues he had received so far: **Intrigued / you should be / you are it / I'm coming / for you / but when / not yet / they're cross words / soon / then where / very near / and why**.

"Father Tim's idea of thinking outside the box seems hopeful to me. But I've tried doing that ever since I saw him a couple of days ago and I haven't gotten very far. I'm hoping that with your help we might come up with something. So do any of you have any ideas now that you've heard what Father Tim gave me?"

After some moments of silence, Pat Kelly spoke up. "Just to be sure: the SUV evidence led nowhere?"

"Right," Father John said. "The sheriff ran through a number of them in the county and got nowhere."

"Have you considered that it might be from out of state?"

"The sheriff and I ruled that out as unlikely because it would be hard to come a long way like that just to keep putting stuff into my paper box ... *hard*, but not *impossible*, I suppose."

"But what if that was the only time an SUV was used?"

"I don't guess either of us thought about that. But tracing that would be like hunting down the proverbial needle in the haystack then, don't you think?" Father John asked.

"Perhaps, but I think you ought to run it past the sheriff anyway," the lawyer said.

"Noted. I'll do that," Father John said and scribbled something on the pad of paper he had before him.

Paul Leubel wanted to know: "Do the Dudenbostels figure into the mix?" He was the one who first reported their presence in town.

Again it was Father John responding: "Not that the sheriff or I can figure. And remember: I talked to Mr. D. in the hospital. He has no roots here in Algoma or the county, he told me. And he seemed very comfortable in our conversation. He's either a very good actor or not at all connected to this. I concluded the latter."

"I still think it's a big coincidence that no clues showed up until after he and his family got to town. Can you check with the Post-Dispatch to see if he was in any way involved with that gimmick of tying a mystery to a crossword puzzle, Father?"

"I can and will, Paul. But my memory says that the originator of the idea was named by the editor and later submitted his own puzzle ... and the name was nowhere near as strange as Dudenbostel. But I'll ask."

"But wasn't another puzzle sent in before the originator of the idea sent his own in? Who sent that one?"

"Good point, Tom. I don't think I ever knew. So I'll check that out too. But even if we find that the Dudenbostels were involved with the Post on the puzzle idea, we're only a tad closer. It doesn't nail anything down. Am I right?" Father John asked.

Pat Kelly said: "Yes, you're right. But that *tad closer* you spoke of would give us a foothold. I'm not sure exactly how we'd pursue things after that, but my legal instincts call that something of a *smoldering* gun ... not a *smoking gun*, if you understand the distinction, however lame it may be."

Tom said: 'I don't get it."

"A smoking gun is evidence that could be used in court. You know, the Nixon thing ... Watergate?" Several of the young men nodded. "By *smoldering gun* I mean to suggest something lesser. We'd have some further work to do if that were the case. It doesn't quite get us there, you know. Forgive the very imperfect metaphor, but I hope you get it now."

"Okay. Thanks," Tom said and grinned. "I'm not up on all my technical legal jargon."

"Have you tried to see if the clues can be made into little crosses, Father?" Harry asked.

"No."

"I'll try to do that. And I'll let you all know if it can be done ... and if it seems to mean anything," Harry volunteered. That got a thumbs up from Father John.

114

"Someone should check out the plague cross on the Germantown-Breese road."

"Why, Willy?"

"Father Tim mentioned it, and I don't think we should overlook it."

"Okay, but what do we look for?"

"I think we check out the wording on it. Maybe something will jump out at us. Who knows, Jim?"

"You want to do that, Willy, since you came up with the idea?"

"Sure. I can do that. And I'll get back to the group if there's anything we can use."

Father John spoke up again. "Lots of you have things to check on, it seems, but I haven't heard any real breakthroughs. Perhaps we ought to just be quiet for a while and each of us mentally play around with the word *cross* to see if something occurs to anyone. That sound like a good idea?" There were nods around the group, and everyone fell silent.

After what seemed an eternity, Harry Grant spoke. "At the risk of bringing something up that sounds Herculean, should we maybe look into all the crosses in and on the churches of the county. We could begin here at Saint Helena's …"

"What are we looking for, Harry?"

"I'm not sure, Tom, but just like the plague cross, maybe there's something on or around one church cross that will make some sense. Does anybody think it's worth a try?"

Father John rushed to his defense. "The task does sound gargantuan, all right. But what else do we have? If some of you are willing to try, what do we have to lose? I can do the Saint Helena's snooping ... "

Pat Kelly jumped in. "I think two people ought to do each church. One can be a devil's advocate to the other. Also less chance, that way, of overlooking something or taking something for granted." That got universal approval and soon teams were formed. Harry would tell Tom that he'd be with him.

"And just like the earlier suggestions, we may not know exactly what to look for, but anything that suddenly grabs somebody should be pursued. I suggest we set a deadline for reporting back here. What about one week? Can you all get one church done in that time ... along with whatever else you each volunteered for? And we all need to keep in mind that somehow this should relate to Father John." Pat put some urgency in his voice.

The group agreed, and with that they decided to break up. Before they left, however, Father John cautioned them to check with the pastors of the churches they would be investigating.

"What do we tell them if they ask why we're wanting to do this?"

"That's a good question, Willy," Pat Kelly said. "I suggest you tell them you're doing some research for a project at Saint Helena's. That's true enough. And if they press you, you could link it to something liturgical."

Father John chimed in. "Not a bad idea, actually. Getting a different crucifix for above our altar isn't out of the question. The parish council's actually looking into that. It wouldn't hurt to get some ideas for that. Maybe you guys will come up with something that *will* actually help us liturgically. And in the meantime, I'll alert our liturgical committee to do some brainstorming too. We'll kill two birds with one stone: cover our tails and maybe get a new crucifix.

"Something else just occurred to me. There are Stations of the Cross in all the churches, and sometimes there are crosses below each one of them as part of the motif. And don't forget the sacristies. You can often find one or more crucifixes there as well.

"You know, it's also a good idea for me to join the troops at breakfast in Germantown over the next several weeks. If anything's brewing I'll be able to head it off at the pass." When several of the young men looked quizzical, Father John explained about the weekly breakfasts most of the county priests shared at a Germantown restaurant. "I'll be able to back up what you tell any of the pastors. In fact, it's probably a good idea to bring up the matter before something needs to be said by any of you in the first place."

All the bases thus seemed covered, and the group finally left for their homes. Father John huddled with Jim Eisner, his partner for Saint Helena's, before he got away. He wanted to know when they could do their investigating. The next evening after Jim's supper with his family seemed the best, so they settled on that.

Father John went to bed that night hopeful again.

CHAPTER 26

Before the group's next meeting, Father John celebrated a wedding, a funeral and a baptism at a weekend Mass. He had also come up with nothing from the crosses at Saint Helena's church. For a brief moment, Jim Eisner thought he had something. "That thingamabob near the bottom of the crucifix in the sacristy, Father, what is that?" he had asked.

"That thingamajig," Father John said in mock correction of his young friend, "is a stand to rest feet on. Sometimes the Romans put one there to allow the criminal to push his body up and relieve the pressure on his intercostal muscles and breathe better, thus allowing the criminal to stay alive longer … and suffering longer," Father John explained.

"So it's not significant for our purposes, I'm guessing."

"I think we can conclude that, Jim."

Their coming up empty had been a disappointment, but a minor one, they hoped. Perhaps the others would find something pertinent.

Meantime, the day before they were to reconvene, another clue showed up overnight. *SOME YEARS AGO.* It made no sense. But the morning of the gathering, still another clue appeared: *REMEMBER ?* And that one threw things into somewhat better focus: *Intrigued / you should be / you are it / I'm coming / for you / but when / not yet / they're cross words / soon / then where / very near / and why / some years ago / remember ?*

When Father John shared this with the group before any of them could report on what they had found, he noted two things. "This is the first time any punctuation mark has been included. Some were implied earlier, but this is the first actual one. And also whatever we're looking for is in the past, or at least refers to the past … not the recent past. Let's keep that in mind in light of anything you may have turned up."

This time Tom was with them in the rectory. Father John made a little joke about how biblical that sounded: Thomas was in the upper room the second time Jesus appeared to them there, but not the first time. Small smiles greeted that. They seemed dutiful to Father John, and he quickly signaled they ought to get on with things.

Harry said he had tried a long time to mess with making little crosses of the words. "It's possible, Father. In fact, it's easy … maybe too easy. But doing so didn't tell me anything, I'm afraid."

None of the teams uncovered anything they thought helpful.

"Well, at least the priests didn't bring up anything in Germantown. I guess they're not a curious lot," Father John said.

"So where are we, then?" Pat Kelly wanted to know.

After a moment of silence, Willy Peters ventured: "Square one?"

Nods around the room signaled agreement with him.

"Well then, what does this latest set of clues tell us? That whatever is sticking in the craw of this person has some age to it? That would seem to be the case," Father John said slowly.

119

The group sat dejectedly for a while. Then Paul Leubel looked up suddenly and said: "Maybe it's not churches we should be poking around in. What if it's something to do with a cemetery? There are crosses there too." The bright look on his face remained while the others processed what he had said. "Come on, think about it. I'm right, not?"

Jim said: "Even so, think about how long tracking down something in even one cemetery would take. And how many cemeteries are there in the county ... not just Catholic ones, either? Good grief, man!"

Father John leaped to Paul's defense. "I hate to think of the work, but Paul may have a point. Maybe something's on a gravestone. We could always start with our own cemetery and see where that leads us ... or doesn't lead us. We can decide later on to continue the search or not."

The looks on the group's faces didn't seem promising.

"It's nearly Thanksgiving, Father. And it's cold. And we could easily get snow soon." That sentiment came from Willy Peters.

Rick Binz had been notably quiet throughout both meetings at the rectory, but he finally spoke up. "We've got a lot invested in this already. I for one don't want to see it wasted. I'm willing to put some time in it."

That eventually swayed the group.

"You've all been incredibly generous with your time. Why don't we give it whatever time we can this Saturday. If that doesn't yield anything, maybe then we give it up. And we want to beat the snow, right?"

Father John's suggestion seemed reasonable, and even Pat Kelly said he'd go along with the idea. So the group would meet at the truck stop for breakfast at eight o'clock the next Saturday morning and go to the cemetery thereafter. Father John said that as long as he had to be back for confessions and Mass by 4 o'clock, none of them should stay any longer than that, and if some had to leave earlier, that would be okay too.

The rest of the week past slowly for Father John, but eventually Saturday morning dawned and by nine o'clock after a truck stop breakfast they were all at the entrance of Saint Helena's Cemetery.

CHAPTER 27

Father John had some initial words before they started to spread out and comb the cemetery's crosses for clues: "Before we split up, here's a diagram Paul has made. I've copied it for each of you, and I've given one to the sheriff as well. Maybe something like it will appear out here. Neither Paul nor I can make out anything helpful from it, but perhaps one of you can. And maybe something like it is to be found out here at the cemetery.

```
                Y O U A R E I T
                O
                U
                S O O N         V
                H               E               T
                S O M E Y E A R S A G O         H
                U               Y               E
                L               N               Y
                D           R E M E M B E R     E
                B               A               C
        I N T R I G U E D       R               R
                M                               O
                C   N                           S
            F O R Y O U                         S
                M   T       A                   W
                I   Y       N                   O
        B U T W H E N       D                   R
                G       T H E N W H E R E       D
                            H                   S
                            Y
```

With that, they split up into pairs, Father John as the odd man out joining Pat Kelly and Jim Eisner. From time to time the members of the three mini-groups contacted each other by cell phone, but by noon no one had come across anything worthwhile.

"Let's grab a sandwich at McDonald's and warm up," Father John suggested. "It's on me." The temperature was in the 40s, but the wind was brisk and after several hours of being out in it, the seven of them were feeling the chill.

Over burgers and coffee, they recounted what they had … and mostly had not … seen. They all agreed that the styles of crosses were more varied than had been expected, but nothing any of the group had come across seemed relevant. Harry summed it up: "I mean, a cross is a cross. Period. End of story!" He had said it in such mock solemnity that he got a laugh from his four buddies — Father John didn't find it funny and Pat Kelly was at the counter for a refill to his coffee and didn't hear Harry's joke.

Father John asked if they wanted to continue. "I'll understand if you don't feel like it," he said.

Jim Eisner spoke for the young men: "It'll only take an hour or two more to finish checking out the other graves. Why not keep going to the bitter end? Who knows? Lightning could still strike."

Pat Kelly excused himself to head back to his office, but the others accompanied Father John back out amidst the headstones. By half past two they had completed their survey of all the graves and still came up empty. Father John thanked them and wearily went back to the rectory to be ready for Saturday confessions and Mass. It wasn't until after he sat down to a spartan supper afterward that another idea came to him.

What if it's not some cross-shaped object that's out there among the graves, but one that isn't *out there?* He had remembered the strange large grave marker that did not have a cross atop it, the

Polish one. Another group had gotten to that one, so he made a mental note to go back out to it when he could find the time.

On Monday morning he was standing by the Polovitski gravesite, which indeed had no cross atop it, though there were bas relief crosses beside the names of the husband and the wife. *I don't know what this proves, but I have a hunch it could be significant. It's just got to be. I wish I could pin down why or in what way.*

He phoned to ask the group for one more skull session at the rectory so he could pass on this new insight and see what they might make of it.

He told them of the tombstone and his observations about it. The first to speak was Pat Kelly.

"You said Mr. Feldspar mentioned a city ordinance about the height of grave markers, right?" Father John nodded. "When was that enacted? And is it still in effect?"

"Not sure about either, Pat. Larry didn't say, except to mention that it was a long time ago. Judging from the date on the wife's grave — 1889 — it must have been around then."

"Do you think there would have been a cross on top of that marker if the ordinance had not limited the height?"

"I do, Pat. It's in the Catholic cemetery, and given the Polish name on the stone, I can't imagine otherwise. That's what gave me this idea."

"Maybe someone's upset about that … enough to harass you over it."

"Maybe, Pat, but I didn't have anything to do with that."

"We all know that, but don't ask for logic if someone's holding a grudge, especially one from that long ago."

"Let's say that's the case. It's got to be someone connected with the Polovitski family then, right? No one by that name is around here now that I know of. We can check the voter rolls in the county, of course, but I'm willing to bet we won't find the name Polovitiski," Father John said, looking frustrated. "Do you think maybe in St. Louis we could find someone by that name?"

"*If* we do," Jim Eisner said, "we fall back on the supposition that no one would come so far to leave this many clues here, right?"

Father John nodded, the fire gone from his eyes and a lot of the hope from his heart.

"Unless," Pat Kelly added, "that's someone's maiden name."

The significance of that took a moment to sink in.

Father John felt suddenly rejuvenated: "That could be it, all right. We'll have to do some checking, though, because off the top of my head, I'm not aware of that maiden name lurking anywhere in the county either. But it could have snuck under the radar. Is there some way to easily check on that, Pat?"

"Not *easily*, but there are ways. Marriage records would be the place to start ... "

"I went through those before, and I found it a chore and a half. But I wasn't looking for maiden names. And this time around I could start around 1870, let's say, just to be on the safe side. That cuts out nearly forty years, so it'll be a bit easier." Father John looked and felt hopeful again.

The lawyer continued his thought: "Of course, you know that even if you find something, there still may be more research needed. We've got to be able to hook that information up to the present, you know."

"Picky, picky, picky," Willy said, smiling. And the group laughed.

"Thanksgiving's around the corner, so I don't know when I can get onto that or how long it'll take. But if — *when* — I come up with something, I'll be in touch," Father John said. "You'll probably all appreciate a break anyway, what with the holiday and all. I hope you can all stay alert, though. You never know what you might stumble onto. But meantime, let me worry about the heavy lifting for however long it takes. Okay?" They nodded in agreement and made for the door.

On his way out, Pat Kelly said he'd find out about that city ordinance. Father John thanked him and the rest of the group as they spilled out onto the church parking lot under a cloudless sky and an enormous, beautiful canopy of stars. The cold, crisp evening air promised winter weather, maybe even snow, by the holiday. But none of that mattered to Father John, who was reinvigorated by these latest developments. He couldn't wait to find time for more research at the courthouse.

CHAPTER 28

Father John was unable to get into the courthouse marriage records before Thanksgiving, and in the meantime another clue showed up: *IT'S TIME.* The person who was leaving them in his paper box had the uncanny ability to avoid the patrol cars that were cruising past the rectory at increasingly shorter intervals.

When the sheriff learned about that, he overruled Father John and put him under much tighter protection. That might guarantee that no new clues would be appearing, but he did it to safeguard the priest's life. Father John was told to inform the sheriff any time he planned to leave the rectory. Apparently these increased efforts didn't escape the notice of the mysterious clue-leaver because on the Saturday after the holiday, Father John received one more clue, but this time it was in the mail. It read: *LOOK OUT.*

Sheriff Toler said simply to Father John: "I rest my case." All Father John could do was sigh. He felt they had come so close to finding out what this affair was all about, and now with the police protection, there didn't seem to be any way for things to play out but violently. Still, as it turned out, nothing happened over the next two weeks, which gave the priest ample time to finally comb through the county marriage records.

But that search led to nothing. Pat Kelly had told him the ancient ruling of the city council was rescinded eleven years after its enactment. Yet there was no mention of the Polish name anywhere in the county records even up into the twenty-first century — Father John had gone through every record since the 1870s.

127

"Nothing! Nada! Zip! Zilch!" he told the sheriff. "I can't believe it. I thought we were finally onto something. Do you think we assumed too much about the cross stuff?"

"Maybe," the lawman told his friend. "But that's often the way it is in my line of work. You run down every possibility the evidence points to, and it doesn't always pan out the way you'd like … sometimes you come up with nothing at all. Police work is generally a whole lot more dull and plodding than people think, or television tends to portray, for that matter. Sometimes you end up just having to wait for something to break. You learn from dealing with criminals that most of the time they make an eventual mistake. They're not as smart as they think they are." The sheriff left unsaid the fact that in this case, waiting could put the life of his priest friend in jeopardy.

His posse of young men plus Pat Kelly were equally disappointed but promised to remain vigilant. They remained unaware of the increased efforts by county law enforcement to protect the priest. "Best they don't know, Father. Loose lips, you know … " Sheriff Toler told him.

But the absence of any new clues seemed to suggest that whoever the perpetrator was, he might somehow have gotten wind of those efforts.

Winter had set in by now, and a bit of snow had fallen around the first of December, though the ground was bare again soon thereafter. Advent had begun and Father John got absorbed in the events of the parish's liturgical season. And all the while, of course, preparations for Christmas were moving ahead as well.

Christmas was Father John's favorite time of year. As much as he liked the fall, the several weeks around Christmas time had always been the most enjoyable. But this year the mysterious clues had cast a pall over the season, and he had trouble getting into the spirit of things, even though by holiday time no more clues had surfaced and no move was made on the person of Father John Wintermann.

All the while he had been dealing with those mysterious clues he had refrained from telling his parishioners about them. Only that small handful of men was in on things, and the group had stayed successfully tight-lipped. So Christmas came and went uneventfully with regard to the mystery. No new clues or insights, no criminal activity or mistakes. Nothing.

The sheriff and Father John kept touch weekly, sometimes oftener. But the matter had dragged on, and by January it was in the doldrums.

Friends like Richard Wurtz and the Beckers at the pharmacy, however, had noticed that Father John hadn't been himself for a number of weeks, and come early January, Fred and Frieda called asking him to stop by.

Father John went there not knowing what they had in mind. But he soon found out how concerned they were. "What are you two up to?" he asked as he entered their pharmacy "Got something new and juicy for me?"

"Hi. Glad you could come over. Not much popping in town, I'm afraid," Frieda said as she approached his table. "Want a drink?"

"A small diet, please. What's so important that I should come here for it?" By that time Fred had joined him and sat down across from him.

"We've been a little worried about you," he said. "You haven't been your usual self for some time now. How's your health? I thought you'd come back from your retreat out west hale and hearty. And you seemed to have done that. But lately I think you've been slipping. Want to talk about it? Or are Frieda and I wrong about things. Or, worse … " he said after a short pause, "… are we overstepping boundaries by bringing this up?" He looked genuinely concerned.

Father John was shocked to see how transparent he had become but thought: *what good are friends if they can't read you like a book … and show concern when you're hurting?*

"I'm fine, physically, thanks for your concern. I'm a bit worried, however, about a few things I'm not at liberty to talk about. It's nothing you can help with. At least, I don't think you can, not at present anyway. But if things don't resolve themselves soon, I may well ask how you might be able to help. Right now, though, nothing, I'm sorry to say. Wish you could, but … no."

That only served to make his friends even more concerned, and Father John could sense that.

"It has to do with something at the parish, and it's a sensitive matter. I hope you can understand."

They nodded, but not wholeheartedly.

Frieda rose to take care of a customer who had just walked in, and Fred shook Father John's hand, promising to always be there for him. "Don't hesitate to ask … whenever."

Father John finished his soda quickly and made his way out of the store. He was grateful that by then his friends were busy with people who had come into the pharmacy.

Out on the street again, he got into his car and was about to head back to the rectory when he noticed Horace Denver's rig entering a nearby alley. He caught up with the junk man and got out to speak to him.

"Hello, Father John. I've been meaning to speak to you. I ain't seen nothing you might be interested in lately. Not 'til today, that is. I spotted a white SUV in one of the neighborhoods. You said you was interested in one. Wantin' to replace your car?"

"No, Horace, nothing like that. Glad you're so observant, though. Whereabouts did you see it? I may want to talk to the owner."

Father John got the neighborhood address and made his way there. He found the white SUV parked on the street … right in front of the Dudenbostel home. He was flustered at the discovery and took a moment to decide what to do. Then he wheeled his car back around and went straight to the jail.

"Sheriff, Horace Denver just put me onto a white SUV. It's parked outside the Dudenbostel house and it doesn't have an Illinois license plate on it. Can't be sure what state it's from, though. I didn't stay long enough to check that. And I'm not sure of the make or model, either. I thought it best to get right over here."

131

"You did right, Father. Come along with me. We're going right over there. Let's see what we can make of it."

In two minutes they were in front of Herman Dudenbostle's home in the lawman's patrol car, and the sheriff was running the Iowa license plate through his system. The car was a Dodge registered in Iowa, and soon he had the whole pedigree of the owner, the make and model of the car and everything but the VIN number, which he decided to obtain so he could run it through the system too. But the car turned out to belong to someone other than the Dudenbostels, someone who lived in Dubuque.

Getting the VIN number had been easier than Father John realized: just look through the corner of the front windshield. It was quickly determined that the car was not stolen; it was two years old and still listed as owned by the original buyer. The next step, Father John was told, was to get plaster casts of the tires, and to do that, the sheriff would have to announce his intentions to the owner and get permission. "Do you think the driver is inside that house, Father?"

"Beats me, Sheriff. I barely met the man of that house and don't know his wife at all, let alone whoever owns that car. Can you go up and announce you intentions just like that?"

"Yes, but if they give me any static, I'll have to get a warrant. I'm putting my deputy on that right now, just in case," he said as he reached again for the microphone on his dashboard.

"Buzz me back when you've got one, Hank. Meantime, I'll sit here watching the place. If I have to do something before you get that warrant, I'll let you know." To Father John he said: "You remember

132

Hank Winstrom, don't you? He was along with us in northern Illinois when we arrested that drug kingpin last spring."

"I do. But do we just sit here now? I mean, what if someone comes out and wants to know what's going on?"

"I'll tell 'em," Sheriff Toler said.

That sounded too easy to Father John, who felt awkward sitting there in the squad car, even though he noticed that the sheriff looked completely relaxed. "Does this sort of thing happen often, Sheriff?"

"Often enough. Why? Are you nervous?"

"As though you couldn't tell! Yes, I am," he said with some emphasis. "There's not going to be shooting or anything like that, is there?"

"Relax, Father. Nothing bad is going to happen. The most that can go down now is that I'll lose the element of surprise. Just sit tight. We're fine here."

Ten minutes later the radio crackled back to life with news of a warrant.

"Good. Bring it over to me as soon as you get it from the courthouse, then stick around here, Hank. Might need some backup."

That didn't sound reassuring to Father John, but the sheriff smiled at him. Once the deputy arrived with the court document ten minutes later, Sheriff Toler took it, pocketed it and got out of the car. He went to the front door of the Dudenbostel residence after telling Father John to stay put.

As the sheriff rang the front doorbell, it occurred to Father John that it might be better if he weren't seen, but it was obviously too late to avoid that possibility. So he scrunched down in the front seat as low as he could without losing sight of what was happening. The deputy got out of his own patrol car then and simply stood visible to whomever might come to the front door.

When the door opened, Herman talked with the sheriff briefly. Then he disappeared inside and soon returned with another man who immediately followed the sheriff out to the white SUV. After a brief discussion at the van, the deputy was summoned, and in a matter of minutes plaster casts were made of its tires. The warrant was apparently not needed. And with smiles all around, the two men retreated inside the house while the patrol cars left to return to the jail.

Father John was full of questions for the sheriff, and the gist of what the lawman told him was that everything had gone down peacefully, and that the Iowan and Mr. Dudenbostel both showed no signs of fear or guilt and were quite cooperative.

"What do you think that means, Sheriff?"

"Either they're good actors or they've not been involved in anything suspicious. We should soon know which."

"But if they're just putting on a good act … " Father John said.

"… then they may try to make a run for it. That's why Hank's going back there and hanging out for a while to see if anything happens. We should be able to quickly compare the tire casts we just made with those we saved from that snowstorm in October. If they match, I'll be back for a very serious talk with one or more people in that house. If they don't, I'll phone to tell them it was a false alarm."

"You make it sound easy, Sheriff."

"Well, I don't know about easy, but it is a rather straightforward set of procedures."

As it turned out, the tire tracks did not match and the sheriff's call was made. But Deputy Winstrom told the sheriff afterward that the tires on that SUV were new. No way to prove there had been any wrongdoing, but in his mind the matter smelled fishy. "I mean," he said, "why are there new tires on a car that's only two years old?"

"So where does that leave us now, Sheriff?" a worried-looking Father John asked.

"We don't have a smoking gun, if that's what you're getting at, Father. Thus far it's sort of no harm, no foul."

"Yes, but if there really is a connection to that vehicle, we've just alerted them that we suspect something, haven't we? And they may have also seen me in your car."

"If that's the case, I suppose they may have learned something, yes … *if* they're guilty. But remember what I said: most criminals aren't all that smart. If they've been up to something, we'll get 'em."

Easy for you to say, Father John thought. *Easy for you to say.*

CHAPTER 29

Paul was at the rectory door the next day with a revised diagram that reflected the two latest clues. "Don't know if this can help, but I thought I'd do one up for everyone."

"Thanks, Paul. I'll make copies and get them around to the gang." After he closed the front door, Father John stared at the diagram, but it made no more sense now than the first one did. Nonetheless he dutifully copied it for distribution.

```
                  Y O U A R E I T
                  O
                  U
                  S O O N         V
                  H               E           T
                  S O M E Y E A R S A G O     H
                  U               Y           E
                  L               N           Y
                  D           R E M E M B E R
                  B               A           E
      I N T R I G U E D          R            C
          M                                   R
          C       N               L O O K O U T
        F O R Y O U                           S
          M       T     A                     S
          I       Y     N                     W
  B U T W H E N   E     D                     O
          G       T H E N W H E R E           R
                  H                           D
                  Y                 I T S T I M E
```

God bless these young men! What would I do without them and their loyalty?

He couldn't get out of his head that somehow the white van had been involved in planting that October clue. But the tire tracks not matching and the Iowa origin of the van didn't seem to fit. Still, finding just such a van outside the Dudenbostel home was too much of a coincidence … finding it anywhere in town, actually, was more than just happenstance. His gut told him that there had to be some significance.

But how do you link it up to something that happened several months earlier? What if those people visit Algoma with some regularity … or if they're related to the Dudenbostels … or if they're in their employ? How do you establish anything like that?

His mind was a jumble of thoughts: too many and coming too fast. *Slow down, John! Make a list and try to put everything into some sort of order!*

He spent the next several hours doing just that. When he finished, he called the sheriff to apprise him of what he had just done and to ask to share the fruits of his labors with him the next day. Sheriff Toler said he'd rather come to the rectory for that, and tomorrow would be fine.

Thus it was that the two old friends were huddled together over Father John's kitchen table looking at the ideas the priest had put onto paper.

"I like your pursuing the possibility of that SUV having been involved in the clue drop last October. I'm also suspicious about that. I'd like to know why you'd need to put new tires on a vehicle that new. And while I agree that using it for all or most of the clues sounds highly impractical, if that van comes to Algoma periodically, it could easily have been involved in leaving *some* of the clues at your place. So then, why might that car be here in town occasionally, you may ask? The most logical possibility is that those people are connected either by business or by relationship.

"But here's the rub. The name on the Iowa car is Starrett, Jim Starrett. No obvious relationship there."

"But," Father John objected, "what if the relationship is through either wife … Dudenbostel's or Starrett's?"

"Good point, Father. What's Dudenbostel's wife's maiden name? It wouldn't be Starrett, would it?"

"Don't know. But I think I know how to find out. They go to church in Burger, Mr. D. told me. I can call Father Edlen and he should be able to tell me that. I assume they've registered over there at Saints Peter and Paul. Can you get the maiden name for Mrs. Starrett?"

"I can probably pull enough strings to come up with that, yes," Sheriff Toler said. "But even if we find some connection on either end, we don't have a smoking gun, you know. We'll still have to prove they're in on this thing. What we'd really need then … maybe even now, before we start digging into family histories … is *why* this is happening, this business of the clues."

"Yes, but one thing at a time, right?"

"Yepper. You're catching on. If you get any better at this, I don't want you running against me next election," the sheriff said, grinning.

"Is there anything else? Are we overlooking something else we could also be working on?" Father John looked eagerly across the table at his friend.

"Not that I can see. But once we uncover anything — and I'm assuming we're going to get lucky — we'll need to sit down again and plot out the next step or steps. We'll almost certainly need some sort of confrontation, and finding the best way for that to go down will require more planning. You know, if this didn't involve you, Father, I'd have dumped everything and moved on long ago. But my curiosity's been aroused, and as I said, this involves a friend of mine. So I'll keep at it to more or less the bitter end, barring some catastrophe that forces me to put all my attention on a different police matter." He smiled at the priest. "And, lest I forget: we need to get hold of each other the moment either of us comes up with something, like a maiden name or anything else. Agreed?"

Father John nodded, then suddenly looked mortified. "I just now realized that I haven't even offered you a cup of coffee. Next time I promise to do better."

"To heck with coffee. Buy me a steak the next time," the lawman said with a smile and rose from the table.

As Father John escorted him to the door, he said: "I'll probably have something about a maiden name for you before you have anything for me. I'll call even if the information doesn't seem to lead anywhere."

Moments later he was on the phone to Burger's Catholic parish. The secretary informed him that Father Edlen was away on his day off and wouldn't be back until later that night.

"Just tell him that I called, and have him give me a jingle tomorrow," he said. *That's soon enough. I can wait that long.*

But a couple of days went by without a return call from Burger, and Father John had gotten so involved with some odds and ends of parish ministry that he had effectively put the idea out of his mind. When the call eventually came, he chided himself for not having thought about it in the meantime, but immediately also realized that had he remembered and bothered the priest with another call, it wouldn't have sounded at all polite. *And I needn't upset him. He might not give me the information I want.*

"Did you take more than one day off this week, Jim?" he said with a grin that his cohort sensed from the tone of Father John's voice.

"Heaven's no. I couldn't get by with that like some of our guys do. Chalk it up to old age: the note got buried on my desk 'til just now. Maybe I can clean up this mess later this week. What can I do for you?"

"Just a small piece of information, if you please. I saw Herman Dudenbostel in the hospital some time back and he told me that he and his wife are going to church at Saints Peter and Paul. I assume you've registered them. Do you mind telling me her maiden name?"

"I can find that for you. But what on earth do you want that for?"

"When I first became aware that they'd moved into Algoma, one of my parishioners thought that the family had roots here. In the hospital Mr. D. said that wasn't the case. So I'm wondering if perhaps *her* family was the one that went way back here in town. But I need her maiden name to check that out." He was proud of that partial truth that enabled him to avoid telling Jim Edlen the overriding reason for his request.

"Sure enough. You must have a lot of time on your hands if you're into that kind of stuff. Here it is, and it's as much a tongue twister as Dudenbostel. She didn't make signing her new name any easier by marrying Herman. It's Polovitski. Two more typically ethnic names you couldn't find if you made them up. Hope that helps."

Father John was barely able to say that it did and thank his fellow pastor before hanging up. It took him several moments to get his composure and quiet his mind after hearing what the Burger pastor had said. When he calmed down, he called the jail.

"You're not going to believe this, Sheriff. I got Mrs. D.'s maiden name, and it's a hot potato. Can you come over soon? We have to talk."

"Give me ten minutes to finish off something here and I'll be right over. You can't tell me on the phone?"

"I can, but I'd rather tell you here."

"See you soon, then. Put the coffee on," he said, grinning.

CHAPTER 30

"I don't know if you get the full import of this, Sheriff," he said once he had poured his friend a cup of coffee. "Polovitski is the name on that monument in the cemetery."

"What monument are you talking about?" The man looked completely befuddled.

"Oh, I forgot. You've not been in on that, have you? I chanced upon a huge gravestone on the Catholic cemetery right next to the city side. It dates back to the late 1800s and has the Polish name Polovitski on it. It has an odd shape, comes to a point and there's no cross to top it off. Odd, since it's Catholic *and* Polish."

"So what?" Sheriff Toler still looked perplexed.

"There are four burial plots, but only one body buried there, that of Danuta, the wife of Anton. They were here in town for a few years at that time. The husband's name is already carved into the stone, and they had two children, so the other slots were apparently for those three.

"When I got Pat Kelly and the five young guys together for our initial brainstorming session, it came to one of us that it was odd there was no cross on top of that grave marker. Pat found out that there was indeed a city ordinance at the time restricting the height of tombstones, just as Mr. Feldspar had thought. This one apparently came in just under the wire, and there was no room for a cross to top it off.

"Even though the ordinance was revoked eleven years later — thanks again to Pat for double checking that — no cross was ever put there. I've put two and two together and am guessing that this might be our smoking gun, especially because Mrs. Dudenbostel's maiden name is not only Polovitski, but she's also named for that deceased woman. It all fits rather nicely: Danuta Polovitski's still carrying a grudge that's well over a hundred years old about her ancestor who was denied a cross atop her grave."

"I got to admit, that does seem to fit together rather nicely. But now, assuming we've stumbled onto the right stuff here, about that confrontation I spoke of the other day … how do you propose we go about that, Father? Because so far all we got is speculation."

"I was hoping that fell under your area of expertise, but since you've thrown the ball into my court, what about this: I go and talk nicely to Mrs. D. about how coincidentally her maiden name matches the one on that gravestone?"

"And then … ?"

"You mean, what do I do if she doesn't take the conversation any further?"

"Yes, but also what do you do if she does take it all the way to angry?"

"Any recommendations?"

"My first inclination is to tell you to have me with you. But I'm guessing you wouldn't want that. It would be the safest thing for you, though, I'm sure you realize. Covers all the possible bases … "

143

"Yes, but it's not the pastorally best thing. If she has something stuck in her craw about that, I'd want to win her over, not win an argument with her."

"Okay, but are you willing to take the risk that might involve?"

Father John thought for a moment, then when his pastoral instincts kicked back in. "I think I have to."

"Well, let's not get carried away. Why don't you gather your brain trust one more time and run that past them. I could be here too. But that's your call."

"I like the idea of getting them together, and yes, I'd like you along for the ride."

"How's about Saturday evening?"

"Fine. Let's make it for 7:30. That should give everyone involved a chance for supper. I'll promise them that we hope to be done in less than an hour. And I'll get back to you, especially if there's a problem with the date or time."

"Good. I'll wait to hear, but I'm in."

After Larry Toler left, Father John made the calls to his 'brain trust' — he liked the term and made a mental note to share it with the six of them when they got together on Saturday. He got commitments from each of them without saying exactly what the meeting would involve.

We're getting somewhere ... at last! I just know it.

CHAPTER 31

Saturday evening found Father John very excited. Each member of his brain trust picked up on it, and Rick Binz mentioned it out loud. "You the cat that swallowed the canary, Father? What's up?"

"If you don't mind, I'd like to wait for one more person. I've asked the sheriff to be with us. He should be here any minute now."

"Sounds like there's been a breakthrough," Willy Peters said, looking around at the others.

But before Father John could comment, the doorbell sounded. "That's surely the sheriff." He went to the door and let the lawman in.

"Welcome, Sheriff Toler," Father John said as much to his latest arrival as for the group's benefit. "The sheriff is already up to speed on things, and he's here in case we need his expertise as we move forward." The group nodded in acknowledgment.

"By the way, you all have a new title, thanks to him. You're now officially my *brain trust*. Bask in the glory of that a few seconds, and then give me your attention," Father John said with a smile.

"The sheriff and I pursued the white SUV lead. I told him I was convinced that it was somehow involved in planting at least one of the clues, and he thought so too … to prove that we had come up with ways to overcome some apparent dead ends. How explain the tire tracks not matching those from October, and why an out-of-state vehicle might be used to plant that clue.

"I put forward some conjectures that sounded plausible to the sheriff. They were *possible* explanations he agreed we should pursue.

What if, I said, there was some business or relationship connection between the Dudenbostles and the SUV owners? He countered that the van owner's name didn't suggest any relationship, and proving a business connection would be next to impossible.

"Next I said, what if it was either the Dudenbostel wife or that of Jim Starrett's — that's the van guy — through whom the two families were connected." He looked over at the sheriff as if to suggest he continue.

"Father John thought he could easily get Mrs. D.'s maiden name from the parish in Burger," Sheriff Toler said. "I said I'd try to get Mrs. Starrett's. He was successful pretty quickly. *I* only got my information a couple of hours ago, but sure enough, that's where the connection is, through the wives."

"But it gets even better," Father John said. "I found out from Father Jim in Burger — where the Dudenbostles are registered as parishioners — that Mrs. D.'s maiden name is Polovitski, the name on that ginormous grave marker in our cemetery. And not only that, but her first name is the same as the lady's who's buried out there, Danuta. It was just too big a coincidence to pass up."

"And I haven't even told you yet, Father, but Mrs. Starrett is also a Polovitski. They're sisters."

Father John said under his breath: *makes sense!*

The older men fell silent and allowed the group to let that piece of information about the maiden names sink in.

"But wasn't there something about a cast being taken last October of a man's shoe, size … what … eleven or twelve? How's that fit in?" Pat Kelly was acting like a lawyerly devil's advocate.

"There was," the sheriff quickly responded. "But I'll bet big money that Jim Starrett wears a size eleven. It'll be easy to check."

"Think about it. What a wonderful opportunity to keep us guessing! A surprise dusting of snow comes along, so why not use the out-of-town van that just happened to be here in town to deposit a clue in my paper box … and have Mr. S. deliver it, leaving clear tire tracks and footprints. Almost certainly no way to trace that stuff, and a wonderful chance to confuse us even more than they had already. 'Let the local yokels think we're stupid enough to leave those tracks … when all the while it's a red herring!"

"That's great, Father. Nice going. But what do we do now?" Jim Eisner looked excited and concerned at the same time. "Wait a minute. Those tire tracks don't match, right?"

"We haven't got that tacked down yet, but there's too much other stuff, too many other indications that we're on the right track," the sheriff said. "We'll iron it all out, don't you worry. Anyway, it's too suspicious that a relatively new van has a second set of tires on it."

"That's why I've asked the sheriff to be here tonight. I — we, he *and* I — want to hear what you all think about our next step or two. I've got some ideas, which the sheriff is not exactly excited about. But first we would like to hear your ideas."

The group was silent for a while, looking back and forth at each other, and the two older men waited more or less patiently for someone to speak. Pat Kelly eventually did.

"We still haven't established that the Dudenbostels planted the clues. We need a way to do that. Are you going to just wait around with night-vision goggles to catch them? Anyway, I'm betting they won't leave any more clues. First off, the last one warned you to *look out*, right? Secondly, they've probably gotten spooked by your having taken a cast of the SUV's tire treads."

Father John nodded in agreement.

"So then, how are you going to make that connection?" I'm still waiting to hear your ideas," Father John said to the group. "Pat raises a pertinent question. The Sheriff and I agree with the sentiment he just expressed. We have to pin it on someone, presumably the Dudenbostels. So how do you think we can do that?"

More silence.

Paul finally said, "You can't just go over there and ask them, so how do you maybe trick them into admitting it?"

Still more silence.

"You could out and out accuse them of it and see how they react."

"Willy, if we do that, they'd probably deny it," the sheriff said. "Then where are we? Maybe the defendant in some lawsuit?"

Finally Pat asked: "Have you thought that out, Father? Our brain trust doesn't seem to have a good approach to it."

"I came up with something, yes. But remember that I already said Sheriff Toler here isn't so fond of it." The sheriff nodded.

"So what is it?" Paul wanted to know.

"I told the sheriff that I didn't want to confront them with a view to proving them criminally to blame or to winning some contest. What I'm thinking of doing is going there and telling Mrs. Dudenbostel that I came across that gravestone and couldn't help but notice that the name on it is the same as hers ... and see how she reacts. Further conversation could spin off the idea that her family had roots here way back when. And I could eventually get to the fact that there's no cross on the monument ... which may well be what this whole affair is about anyway."

"Yeah, Father, but what if the conversation doesn't play out that way?" Rick Binz asked.

"That was my concern, Rick," the sheriff said. "So I suggested that if Father John was bound and determined to go to her place like that that I should go along. He didn't like that idea."

Pat Kelly spoke the obvious: "Sure would be safer that way."

The sheriff looked at Father John as if to say *I told you so.*

"But it would almost put her into a corner with no way out, the priest said. The presence of the law would strongly suggest that she was in legal trouble, and I don't want that."

"But isn't it a criminal thing we're dealing with ... or at least something bordering on the criminal? Those notes, I mean."

"I suppose you can read it that way, Jim," Father John said, "but if the issue is that I'm being threatened, there's been no *overt* threat yet, and I don't want to push them into making one. If Mrs. D. is upset about that cross issue, there's a fairly easy solution to that. Anyway, there'd be time enough in any conversation with her to explain about that city ordinance and how it got revoked *years ago*. It's a simple thing to put a cross atop that gravestone now."

Pat Kelly spoke up. "I don't know. Let's assume that it is the Dudenbostels who are behind this and you expose that by talking with the lady. Whoever did this went to a whole lot of trouble to drag this out in such a way as to pretty obviously want to punish you, Father, or scare you … or both. Do you honestly think she'll roll over that easily and let bygones be bygones?"

"I can't be sure, Pat. But I can let her know I'm not taking it so much to heart that I want to punish her now that it's come to light."

"How'd you put it to me, Father?" Sheriff Toler asked. "You wanted to be pastoral about it?"

"Yes, Larry, I did put it that way."

"That may well fit your style and your profession. Where I come from, I approach things a little differently. And besides, I'm more than a bit worried. But as I've said before, this is your call. I just hope I don't have to say sometime down the road that I told you so."

The group had become quite sober, and Father John spoke up to bring things to some sort of conclusion. "That's how I'd like to approach matters … unless you all think otherwise … and can convince me there's another, a better, way."

"I'm leery, Father," Pat Kelly said. "I tend to think like the sheriff, I guess. But … if that's how you want to play it, I say go for it.

I just would feel better if there were some safety net for you." Turning to the sheriff, he asked: "Does anyone know if there's any history of violence in the Dudenbostel family?"

The sheriff shook his head. "Haven't a clue. But if I were to guess, I'd say there's probably nothing there to give great cause for concern. But you never know. And those clues did use language that can be taken as alarming."

More silence. Then Father John said: "I can't stop you from hovering outside their house, Sheriff, while I go in to talk. I know that won't give you the kind of certainty you probably want, but I offer that as a compromise."

"I'll take any concessions you're willing to offer, Father. But I'll register my objections like a good attorney in court." He looked at Pat Kelly, who nodded back gently in his direction.

On that somber note the group broke up. The sheriff was the last one out the door, and he paused to ask when Father John was going to talk with Mrs. Dudenbostel.

"Tomorrow, if that's okay with you. I mean, I'll call her tomorrow and I hope I can see her right after that. I'll let you know whatever shakes out."

The sheriff nodded and continued on to his car, but he didn't look to be a happy camper.

151

CHAPTER 32

The call was placed the next morning right after Mass. Danuta Dudenbostel answered the phone.

"Hello, Mrs. Dudenbostel. Would you mind if I stopped past your home for a few minutes for a pastoral visit?" *How could she refuse that?*

"Well, if it won't take very long, that would be okay. I've got to take my little dog to the vet this morning. I assume you mean to come right now ... "

"Yes, that's what I had in mind. I hope your dog isn't ill?

"Oh, no ... it's just time for her regular shots. We'll have fifteen minutes or so, depending on when you get here. Will that work?"

He assured her that it would. When he hung up he called the sheriff, who said he'd make sure to be in the neighborhood. "Be careful, Father."

The lady of the house met Father John at her door. She was holding a small dog. "Come in, Father. We've never met before," she said, stating the obvious.

"So this is whom you're taking to the vet, eh? What's her name? You did say the dog was a 'she,' didn't you?"

"She's Mitzi."

"May I pet her?"

"Yes. She's very friendly."

Father John followed the lady into the living room and took a seat on the sofa. She sat opposite him in an overstuffed matching chair.

"I suppose you know I met your husband in the hospital. I trust they got his medications satisfactorily adjusted."

"Yes. His diabetes doesn't appear to be that severe. He's managing it well, thanks to his doctor. The only problem is that he may not be here that much longer. They rotate people at places like Scott with some regularity."

Father John wondered if that was true of civilians. "Oh, so his doctor is in the military then? He told me about working at Scott Field."

"Yes, he does, and he likes the internist he met there."

"If he has to find another doctor, we have several here in the area that are good. And there are others in Belleville. A couple of them are friends, in fact. He might want to sniff out the reputations of some of these so he can easily make a shift if he has to."

"I'll mention that, although Herman's almost certainly ahead of that game. He usually is."

"Well, I realize that you're under some time constraints Mrs. Dudenbostel … "

"Please call me Dannie, Father."

"Thank you, *Dannie*," he said. "But since you need to get away shortly, let me get right to what brings me here. I had occasion to notice a very large grave marker in our cemetery recently. Mr.

Feldspar from the mortuary told me a bit about it when I spoke of it to him during a burial.

"When I checked further, I noticed its peculiar design: no cross atop it, I mean. I also noticed it belonged to a family named Polovitski. I wasn't aware of any Poles here in the parish, so I checked our records and found just that family from the cemetery in all our history. Then when I learned somewhat later from Father Jim over in Burger that was your maiden name, I couldn't help wondering whether you're related to the lady buried here. Especially since your name is exactly the same as hers."

"Yes, Father. All that is true. Why?"

"I just thought you might not know why there's no cross atop the gravestone. I have a theory about that, but I also have been wondering if you might want to remedy that. If you do, I know a good monument dealer near the bottom of the state whom I'd be happy to recommend to you."

"How thoughtful of you. The story is a long one, I'm afraid and, as I said, I'm in something of a rush. Perhaps another time?"

"Oh, certainly. Should I phone you or would you prefer to call me?"

"I can be in touch, Father."

"'Til another time, then, Dannie," Father John said as he stood to take his leave. "I hope that will be soon."

They exchanged smiles, and moments later the priest was outside. He caught sight of the sheriff's car idling down the street, and without acknowledging its presence, got into his own car and pulled away. But he put his Taurus on a path toward the jail and noticed in his rearview mirror that the sheriff was following him.

When they sat down with some coffee inside his office, the sheriff was eager to know how things had gone inside the Dudenbostel residence.

"Extremely polite. You wouldn't think there was anything amiss at all or that she and her husband were up to anything with regard to me."

"Nothing threatening, subtle or otherwise?"

"Nothing anyone could even remotely view as suspicious."

"What do you make of that, Father?"

"She's a cool customer. But then, I gave her nothing to be upset about. I told her what I knew about the grave marker, that I figured it belonged to her ancestors and that I knew something about why there was no cross on it. Then I said I could link her up with someone to fix that. A monument dealer near Cairo is a friend of mine, actually, and I can indeed put the two of them together if she wants that."

"So why was your conversation so short? There was nothing untoward about her shooing you out of her house?"

"Not at all. She told me on the phone that her dog was due at the vet's. Apparently there was an appointment she was loathe to blow off. Or it was a convenient excuse."

"So … it was amicable."

"Extremely polite, as I said."

"You gonna get back with her, then?"

155

"So she says. I'm to wait for her call."

"Are you satisfied with all this? I'm guessing that you aren't."

"It's rather more like so far so good … more to come!"

"Can you be patient?"

"For a while, yes. But I'm no babe in the woods, Sheriff. If there's been a threat to me, I'm not out from under that. But the game has definitely gotten more interesting. We'll have to see how this plays out."

"I agree, so I'm not backing off from the protection I've activated for you. And I still say you need to watch your back."

Father John was smiling as he left the jail. But a quote from Chester A. Riley, on the old radio drama, *The Life of* Riley, occurred to him: *What a revoltin' development this has turned out to be.*

CHAPTER 33

However he had expected his conversation with Danuta to turn out, what actually occurred wasn't even close. Father John couldn't be sure if she was very cool and calculating or if he had gotten her curiosity up and she really wanted to hear him out about the gravestone. Time would tell. But he was willing to bet that there would be no more clues for him outside his back door. *They're too spooked by now for that. But how real a threat the Dudenbostels pose remains to be seen.*

He wasn't sure she would really call him, but within a couple of days he did hear from her. "I have to come uptown to do some shopping, Father. Should I stop at the rectory?"

He recovered from his mild surprise quickly enough to suggest that they meet at the pharmacy instead. "I have to get some things there anyway, and it'll be more convenient for you, I presume, to meet there. Is that all right?" *If she's up to something, I'll be safer in a public place.*

It was, she assured him, and accordingly they were huddled in a booth near the back of the drugstore by two o'clock. After Father John ordered soft drinks for each of them, he spoke.

"You had said it was a 'long story' about that gravestone, Mrs. Duden … ah, excuse me, Dannie," Father John said, looking at her expectantly.

"It is indeed. And I'll tell it to you. But first, I'm curious as to why you're so concerned about it. I can't imagine that it's anything to you but a very old grave marker in your cemetery."

"I'm probably an atypical parish priest, Dannie. For this old German, that piece of marble represents a loose end, something that could, perhaps should, be taken care of. Mind you, I'm not about to shell out what little money I have to take care of that, but when I discover someone who's connected to it, I immediately think about seeing if he or she wants to do it for me. It's one of my many quirks, I suppose, but if you want a cross there, Dannie, and are willing to pay for putting it there, I'll feel better. I don't know if you can understand that twisted thinking, but it's one of the ways my mind tends to work."

"If you say so, Father. But let me tell you what I know about that tombstone. My great-grandfather came over here from Gdansk in the mid-1860s. He and my great-grandmother were already married but didn't have children yet. Two would eventually come after they got to southern Illinois. They ended up first in Chicago for several years and then made their way down to Algoma, where he planned to make a living by farming.

"When his Danuta died of influenza, he reluctantly took his two children back to Chicago, where he got work with the city as a laborer maintaining the city streets. It turned out to be a good civil service job, one that could adequately take care of his family. He remarried soon thereafter to have a mother for his children and died there. His son was my grandfather and lived and died in the city also. I was born there to his son, who was also named Anton, and after I met Herman, I moved away from the city, going with my husband from place to place as his work with the Air Force dictated.

"When he was recently offered a civilian job at Scott, and we realized we were going to be living in the vicinity of my great-grandfather's one-time home, we zeroed in on Algoma, liked what we saw and moved here. That's not a very exciting or even complicated story, but it's mine."

She had spoken rather rapidly and ended up sounding a bit out of breath. When she finished, it sounded to Father John as though she wouldn't have much more to say. He also sensed that she had said her piece without really telling him all that she might have had to say and wasn't going to be easily prodded into adding to it without a good reason.

She may or may not want to hear what I know about that cross-less stone, but she's certainly cool.

"Thanks for that mini-autobiography, Dannie. You said your grandfather *reluctantly* went back to Chicago. Why reluctantly?"

"Well, among other things, he had two children and no mother for them. Not even the promise of one, not here *or* in Chicago. But he surely couldn't raise the kids *and* run a farm at the same time … and he had more connections in Chicago than here, that's for sure. So he went back, even though his heart was really here on the farm. He was a tenant farmer at the time but had aspirations to own the land. He had, after all, come from farming roots in the old country. It was what he knew best and loved most."

When she finished, Father John still had the feeling that there was more to the word *reluctant* than what she had said, however plausible her story sounded. She had, after all said that *among other things*, this was his story.

"Of course" was all he said in response to her. But then he added: "You probably want to know what I've learned about the absence of a cross on the gravestone." She nodded without speaking.

"It turns out that Algoma had in place an ordinance dictating how high gravestones could be. It was subsequently revoked a little over ten years later, but when Danuta died it was still very much in place. Perhaps your great-grandfather wasn't aware of that city mandate before he purchased what must have been a rather expensive monument for his wife's grave.

"I noted the clever design, by the way, which allows for four burial plots: one for Danuta, one for himself — his name is on the marker, as I'm sure you know — and two others, presumably the two children. That tells me he intended to stick around here, as you seem to indicate. That he moved away tells me he left before that ban disallowing anything higher atop the headstone was rescinded.

"But *you* can easily rectify things and put a cross on top of the stone, as I have to believe he would have wanted. That is, if you are equally inclined.

"Mind you, I'm not suggesting that you should or must, merely that you can. It matters not all that much to me either way. But someone such as yourself, a member of the family, may think it important enough to do something like that. And I wanted to be sure you knew that background and especially the fact that you're entirely free to alter that stone now and thereby fulfill your deceased relative's presumed wishes." All the while he was closely watching her face. She didn't betray any of her thoughts while he spoke.

"Thank you, Father, for that history lesson. I think my grandfather always thought the restrictions were from the local parish. The grave, after all, is in the Catholic cemetery ... so the story went any time I ever heard my father and grandfather tell it, at any rate."

So, there's the rub, Father John thought, *or at least one of the rubs!* Aloud he asked: "Your great-grandfather then was aware of that ruling, but thought it was from the church and not the city?"

"Oh, yes, precisely. *Very* much aware."

And the story was often told in the family too. It really must have been a bone in Anton's throat ... and surely another reason for getting out of Dodge to go back to the big city. In fact, it remained contentious through several generations, apparently, even to this day.

"I meant what I said at your home, Dannie, about knowing a good monument dealer, a very honest one. He's in business in a little town near Cairo. He's done my gravestone, incidentally. Anyway, I'd be glad to have him contact you, or tell you how to get hold of him, should you ever want to do something about Anton's and Danuta's stone. I just know how important it is to my parishioners to get just the right gravestone for their loved ones. I assume that to be the case with most Catholics."

She had given no indication about that matter or anything else that Father John had been saying for the past few minutes. She didn't even grace his last little speech with a thank-you or any other indication she had heard or approved or was grateful for it.

161

In the awkward moment that followed, Father John made a show of finishing his diet soda by slurping loudly through his straw and volunteering that he had errands to run. They stood, she offered a perfunctory thank-you for the soda and the chat, and they parted.

Father John went to pay Frieda and left. Danuta Dudenbostel was still sitting in the booth at the back of the store nursing her drink when he went through the front door.

Outside, he suddenly remembered that he had wanted some mouthwash, but found it awkward to go back inside to get that now. It would in all probability send a wrong message to the lady in the booth. So he made for home and more pondering about the enigma that Danuta Dudenbostel was proving to be.

CHAPTER 34

On his way home he stopped at the jail. He waited ten minutes for Larry to get off the phone but collected his thoughts in the meanwhile. By the time the two were face to face, they were sipping coffee and the priest was able to put things succinctly to the lawman.

"I can't escape the suspicion that however much I'm gradually burrowing into the core of her story — and I think I'm definitely making progress — there's still more, a lot more, a *crucial* amount more she's not telling. The lack of a cross on the tombstone is definitely an issue in her family, a big one. But there's more. I can sense it.

"For one thing she hasn't warmed to me or to any of what I've told her. I've all but said that the priest wasn't the problem for her great-grandfather — that's how Anton is connected to her. And I've offered her a good way to put a cross on top of the gravestone out there to rectify that old grievance. But she didn't even thank me for that and has instead remained very icy.

"In fact, she's icier now than ever. I saw her just now in Becker's, and she was barely polite. She listened, all right, and didn't pull a gun or threaten me in any way ..." He looked at the sheriff with the tiniest of grins on his face at the irony. " ... but I wouldn't call her reaction, or lack of one, really, something I should be happy about."

The sheriff assumed a thoughtful pose, and Father John waited for him to speak. "How are you going to get her to talk about those clues?"

"Frankly, I'd hoped to soften her up with this gravestone chitchat. I thought the issue wasn't running as deep as I now fear it is. If she's deeply bent out of shape about that damned tombstone, I may not get her to voluntarily 'fess up, let alone back off those implied threats. She just may be very serious about retribution. I'd still like her to talk about that, though, but I'm not sure how to bring her around. I guess I'll hold out hope *for a while* that what we've spoken about so far will slowly melt her. But if not, I'm totally unsure where to go. You got any ideas?" He looked hopefully at the sheriff.

"Sorry, buddy, but I don't. Remember, we've been playing in your ballpark. My approach would be a lot more blunt and hard-core. You didn't seem to favor that earlier. Have you changed your mind?"

"If by hard-core you mean rush in with a view to arrest her, then no, I haven't. But I must admit, her reactions so far can easily be interpreted as strongly leaning toward punishment, and if that's the case, she may be on the verge of something criminal." He thought for a moment, then said: "That's scary."

"Yep. We're playin' hardball, I'm afraid. But keep trying. You may pull it off your way yet. I hope so … for your sake, Padre. Oh, and by the way: you keep talking about *her*. Is there a role for Mr. D. in this? Or do you think Herman's totally on the sidelines?"

"I can't be sure, but my gut says he's not part of this. Until I see otherwise, I think it's all Dannie girl."

"Well, ride 'em, cowboy! Take it as far as you can. Just be careful. I'll try to keep you covered."

Father John nodded his assent and headed outside to make for the rectory and another evening of anguished second-guessing. By bedtime he didn't feel he had made any headway, but he put it in the hands of the Lord and resolved to continue with the matter in the morning.

CHAPTER 35

The next morning Saint Helena's pastor decided that the Lord hadn't been as good overnight as he sometimes is. Father John awoke after fitful sleep and with nothing to show for it but a tired feeling. Still he redoubled his efforts to focus on being prayerful at morning Mass and returned afterward to the rectory for oatmeal and toast.

He decided that the best strategy was to get busy with other things and allow the Spirit to work on his subconscious in Her own way and at Her own speed. By noon he felt better. He had cleared off most of the clutter on his desk, made several phone calls and made a decision to tell the brain trust how his meeting with Mrs. D. had gone. But instead of calling a meeting, he opted to collar them after whichever of the weekend Masses any of them attended. If he had to go over the same story three times, that would be okay.

He felt the Germantown Thursday morning convocation of pastors beckoning him, so the next day he joined his friends for breakfast there. Again the Lord let him down. The gathering was enjoyable, but nothing insightful or earthshattering surfaced. Not, that is, until they had finished, when Jim Edlen walked up to him by his car before he could pull away.

"I didn't want to say anything in front of the others, John, but I got a disturbing call from Danuta Dudenbostel yesterday. She complained to me for sending you over to her house last week."

"But you didn't do that, Jim."

"You know that and I know that, but apparently she thinks otherwise. Did you go to her home?"

"I did …"

Before he could finish his sentence the Burger pastor cut in: "Why? What did you do or say there?" He sounded upset.

"Cool down, Jim. I told her about a family tombstone in our cemetery. It dates back to the late 1800s. There's no cross atop it, and I told her I knew why that was probably so. It was because of a silly city ordinance at the time prohibiting cemetery stones higher than … I don't know the exact figure, but obviously this one came close to the limit.

"I discovered in that conversation that I was right in assuming it was a bone of contention in her family, what with no cross and all, and I thought she'd be happy to know that the ordinance was revoked soon thereafter, and she could do something about that stone, if it was so all-fired important to her family. I didn't phrase it that way, of course. The conversation was polite … on both our parts.

"And a good part of our conversing took place at Becker's a few days later. And she *voluntarily* joined me there. She was in a hurry that first day and we couldn't finish. So I haven't the foggiest about why she'd be upset. She didn't appear so on either day while I was with her."

"Well, she was. But from what you say, I can't imagine why either. Anyway, she said something about not being sure she and her husband would be attending Saints Peter and Paul any more."

"Well, if she's been driven away, it appears to me that it's her own doing, Jim."

"From what you say, it could well be. I'll let you know if she's there next Sunday or not. That's when they usually come, Sunday mornings. It's something about her not thinking Saturday is a 'right' or 'proper' time to satisfy her Mass obligation."

That sounded pretty rigid to Father John too, but he kept quiet about it. From the look on Jim's face and his tone of voice, he didn't seem to agree with that sentiment any more than Father John did.

"Is there something you want me to do about it, Jim?"

"No. I guess not. If she had problems with the conversation you just described, your talking with her again can hardly be helpful." Father John had to agree, but he had asked because of his friendship with his fellow pastor, and also because Jim *might* have had something in mind for him to do about the matter.

When they parted, Jim seemed to have lost any negative feelings he may have felt at first, and Father John was relieved about that.

But here was a whole new dimension to l'affaire Dudenbostel. It would seem at first glance that her anger was as misplaced in this instance as it it had been these many years over the tombstone. *What are we dealing with here? Can there possibly be any rapprochement with someone who is governed so easily by negative feelings rather than by reasonable thoughts?*

"Good question," Larry Toler said when Father John explained what he just learned from Jim Edlen and posed his unspoken question to his law enforcement confidant. "Good question! Are you ready to play the game in my ballpark now?"

"No, but I surely feel the need to talk about this with you."

"For starters, she sounds exactly like the kind of person who can go to extremes to avenge some real or imagined slight."

"Unfortunately, because I hate to give you any ammunition for your argument," Father John said sheepishly, "I agree with you on that."

"And in my book that makes her clearly dangerous."

"You don't see any possibility of her getting it all out of her system and settling down to be a human being again, do you? Oops, that's too strong. But you know what I mean. I hope."

"Well, let's just say that if I were a betting man, I'd not put any money on that possibility," the sheriff said smugly.

"So you think she's a psychopath?"

"I didn't say that."

"A sociopath, then?

"No again. There you go overstating things once more."

"But you don't trust her."

"Now, *that's* a safe assumption. Look, we can't be sure how invested she is in any literal interpretation of those clues she appears to have left for you. But we do know she's upset about something, at least part of which seems to be that tombstone. We also know she's jumped to several conclusions, or better yet, has twisted some things to favor her smoldering anger. Beyond that it's not wise to speculate.

"However, some serious yellow flags have popped up here and we've got to be very careful … more careful even than before."

"What's that mean on my end, Larry?"

"I'd stay away from her, if I were you."

"And if she approaches me?"

"I guess then you talk with her. But I'd be extremely delicate about what you say and do and about how you deal with her. She may just be hankerin' for a fight. Could be that anything you say or do is going to get taken out of context to continue fueling her anger."

"Doesn't sound like the odds in my favor are very good."

"You could say that. And another thing. I'd get me a lawyer. You think Pat Kelly would help you out?"

"I'd say so. And I couldn't do any better. You think she'd sue me?"

"I've no idea, but what's the harm in being prepared?"

"I got your point. Thanks. I'll keep in touch. Right now I think I'll go hunt down Pat."

Father John found his friend in his office. It took the better part of fifteen minutes to brief him on why he thought it prudent to consult him, and then he asked him formally to take his case.

"I suppose you want this to be pro bono," the lawyer said, smiling.

"I'm not in the mood for humor, Pat. Excuse me."

"Sorry. I understand. Sure, I'll represent you."

"I hope that includes advising me too."

Pat nodded and rolled his eyes as if to say *of course.*

"Thanks, my friend. I don't know what we've bitten off here, but it looks like a real snake pit."

"We'll get through it. Just make sure she doesn't come at you with any lethal weapons." Seeing the look in the priest's eyes, he added: "I'm serious, unfortunately."

"I didn't need to hear that, Pat. On the other hand, I guess I did. I'll stay in close contact."

The rest of the day was an uneasy one for Father John. And the night was equally unsettling.

CHAPTER 36

His words to the remaining five members of his brain trust after the weekend Masses unsettled each of them. He tried to look nonchalant and brave, but they saw right through him, and each of them wanted to know how he could help. He told them he wasn't sure but he would stay in close contact. And each young man echoed Larry Toler's warning to be careful. Father John's rejoinder was that they should pray for him. But had any of them asked him, he would have admitted that he was nowhere near as brave or optimistic as he let on.

The week progressed with nothing new on the Dudenbostel front until Wednesday. At ten o'clock that morning Father John received a call from Jim Edlen. "Do you have a moment, John?"

"Sure. What's on your mind, Jim?"

"I'm pretty sure you're going to be as surprised about what I'm about to say as I am. I hope you're sitting down."

"You sound peculiar. Are you all right, Jim?"

"Oh, *I* am, more or less, but I'm not so sure you will be in a few moments. I'm sitting here with Herman Dudenbostel, and after I explain something, he'd like to talk to you."

Father John had been standing by the phone but on hearing that, decided to sit. His friend had already worried him even before anything else he might have to say.

"Herman is upset and worried about his wife. I'll let him tell you exactly, but suffice it to say that he's afraid for her and even more afraid for you. Can he speak to you? He can better explain what's bothering him than I, and I don't want to waste any more time, his or yours."

"Of course, Jim. Put him on."

"Hello, Father?"

"Yes, Herman. The last time we spoke, you were in the hospital. I hope your health is okay."

"It is, Father. But that has nothing to do with my call. I've been very worried about my wife for more than a week now, and every day more so. I couldn't put off doing something about it any longer, so Father Edlen and I have been talking here for more than an hour, since right after morning Mass. He thinks I need to see you."

"He's not been able to help you?"

"Oh, he's been very helpful, the soul of concern, really, but the problem is such that I absolutely do need to talk to you. You see, I have very good reason to think you are in danger ... "

"From what?" Father John couldn't help but cut in to ask.

"More like from whom, Father. From my wife. Dannie has absolutely not been herself for some time now. I'm frightened more each day, actually. She's been slowly turning into something I've never seen before and couldn't in a million years have predicted. She's withdrawn, sometimes spacey and more and more obsessed with her great-grandfather and his wife's grave. And her sister from Dubuque gets mentioned too, although whenever she speaks of her I can't make sense of the ramblings ... "

"Pardon me, Herman, but you've blindsided me with all this and I have to say that *you're* not making much sense to me. Perhaps if you slow down and start over … "

"Oh, Father, I'd be glad to tell you everything. But I don't think over the phone is best for that. May I come to see you?"

"Certainly. Do you mean to come now?"

"Yes, if I may."

"Of course. I'll be waiting."

"There's just one concern, though, Father. My wife thinks I'm at work, which is ordinarily where I'd be this time on any weekday. I've taken a personal day to deal with this, and I don't want to chance her accidentally seeing my car outside your rectory. Might we meet somewhere else … somewhere not in Algoma?"

"Tell you what, Mr. Dudenbostel. Why don't I move my car outside and leave the garage door up. You can drive here and pull right into my space. I'll be waiting for you and can put the door down behind you as soon as you arrive. Then we can talk for as long as you wish right here at the rectory. Would that work?" There was a pause before the man offered a hesitant *yes* to Father John.

"But may I please speak to Father Jim before you hang up, Herman?"

Herman handed the phone back to the Burger pastor and Jim's voice came on the line. "Yes, John?"

"When we hang up, send him on his way and then please call me right back after he's out of your place. Okay? Just give me a few moments to move my car. I'm going to have him park inside my garage."

"Certainly. And thanks for being willing to talk to him." With that he hung up.

Father John immediately put his car into the driveway and returned to his desk, having left the garage door agape. He sat there a minute or two before the phone rang. When it did, he quickly picked it up. "Yes. Is this Jim?" It was.

"Let me ask you about his mental state, Jim. He sounded very agitated. What can you tell me that will be helpful before he gets here? We've got ten minutes, maybe."

"I'd say, yes. He was at Mass this morning and acting very jittery even there. I was surprised to see him in church, it being a weekday and all. He should have been at work. Besides, he and his wife did not show up for Mass this past weekend. And now here he comes today without her. Anyway, he came into the sacristy as quick as he could after Mass and wanted to talk, so we went to the rectory. I've been with him ever since. And, yes, he's agitated. That's one way to put it, though it may be too weak a word. He's very upset, and from what he told me, he has good reason to be.

"I'm no counselor, John. But I know enough to realize he needs one. He also probably needs police assistance. The real problem as he tells it — and I believe him after hearing him out this long — is his wife."

"Good grief, Jim."

"I'll say. But there's more. We don't have time to go into much of what he told me. He'll be at your place soon. He can fill you in on that. But let me say this much. He is convinced his wife is up to no good with regard to you. She wants to do you bodily harm. He can explain all that, but I think you need that forewarning. If I were in your shoes, I'd want to know that."

"Am I safe with him here, alone as I am right now? My secretary's not here today."

"Oh, that part'll be okay. You have no reason to worry about *his* harming you. It's just that what he's going to pour out to you is shocking, and you need to be prepared, that's all. But before it's all over, you may well want to bring the police in on this."

"Are you saying I should call them now?"

"Oh, no. Don't do that. He needs to be alone with you so he can tell you everything. He may clam up if any police were there. But I think you'll want to bring them in when the two of you are finished. And if you do, it'll have to do with his wife, not Herman.

"Anyway, hear him out. I'm going to sit tight here and stay out of everything for the time being. But, please, call me when you two are finished and he's gone. I want to be sure everything's okay with you."

"I promise. Thanks for the heads-up, Jim ... *and* for the concern. I'd better get out to the garage now so I'm there when he arrives. He doesn't want his car to be seen by his wife in case she's out and about."

"I understand. I'll be waiting to hear back. And I suspect your conversation will take a while. If for some reason you can't get me here, don't leave a message. Use my cell phone, instead, and if that doesn't get me, you *can* leave a message on *it.*"

Father John promised to call, then hung up and immediately made his way to the kitchen and the door that leads from there to the garage.

CHAPTER 37

It took a minute or so for Herman's car to show up, but when he finally pulled it into the rectory garage, Father John lowered the overhead door immediately, and Herman emerged looking agitated in the extreme.

"Hello, Herman. Please come inside. I brewed coffee earlier. Would you like some?"

"That would be good, Father. Thanks for seeing me like this."

Father John poured them each a cup and asked about cream.

"Black is fine, Father."

Coffee in hand, they went into the living room and plopped down into large, overstuffed chairs. Father John spoke first. "You said on the phone that yours was a *long story*. Why don't you take your time and tell it to me? I have all day."

Herman took time to compose himself and, with an only slightly less disturbed look on his face, began surprisingly firmly. Sipping occasionally from his coffee mug, he launched into his tale.

"What has emerged recently, Father — perhaps longer than the past few weeks, but very clearly in these past two — was a side of Dannie I'd never seen before. I'd always known her to be sweet, accommodating and very gentle. But lately she's gotten solitary, intense, single-minded to a fault and just plain mean. Mean in her language, mean in her attitudes to other individuals as well as groups, and mean to me as well. She's become demanding, inconsiderate and focused on a narrowing number of things, like that family tombstone in the cemetery here in Algoma, but also certain political and social issues. She's very critical now about a lot of religious things, about our neighbors and their habits, even several relatives who live in Chicago, Iowa and St. Paul. There's more, but that much should tell you that she's become a very unlikable woman ... not like the person I married, by a long shot."

Father John excused himself for interrupting: "What brought this on, do you think?"

"I'm coming to that. But some of what I'm about to say has only begun to make sense in hindsight. It wasn't so clear until lately. I think she's been up to something for quite some time, but I didn't realize it until her personality showed this whole new, darker side.

"We had a visit from her sister and her husband back in October. They were with us for a few days, and things were going along swimmingly. But the night we had that surprise snow shower, she suddenly got the bright idea that our brother-in-law should help her play a practical joke on someone. That's all I knew at the time; I wasn't in on exactly what he was to do or why. But apparently she had him use his big van to leave something at someone's house. I realize now that I never heard anything afterward that might have resulted from that prank, and I frankly forgot all about it until these past few weeks." Father John winced, but kept silent.

"I gather that you came over to our house recently. I didn't learn of that 'til some days later, after she told me she saw you a *second* time shortly after ... at the drugstore here in town. She wouldn't tell me what transpired between you two, but after that

179

second time her transformation became quite evident. Perhaps, as I said, something had been going on inside her for a much longer time, I can't be sure. But after that moment with you she became the Bride of Frankenstein."

Father John's face must have registered the surprise and shock he felt at that moment, because Herman stopped talking and stared at him. "Are you okay, Father?"

"I think so. It's just that those are strong words, Herman. I had no inkling during our conversations that she was in such a stage of upheaval as you describe. She gave no evidence of that either time we talked."

"As I said," Herman continued, "I don't know what went on, but she certainly came back from that an outwardly different person. When I got home that evening from work, she was mumbling angry stuff about all sorts of things, only some of which I was familiar with and none of which I could comprehend. When I tried to get some sense from her, she withdrew emotionally. I just remember that night as a very unsettling one.

"By the next evening when I got back from Scott, she was more willing to talk, but while I understood her words, her logic was elusive at best. What was clearest was her intense anger. Maybe she had bottled so much stuff up inside for so long but that evening it all started to pour out. It was jumbled and I had trouble following it. It took the next week before a clearer picture emerged.

"Several things seem to have coalesced into a perfect storm inside her. In no particular order these include her ancestor's tombstone; her Polish heritage that seems to have given her a rigid approach to life — more rigid than I had ever been aware of — and to religious morals *plus* an inferiority complex; and some until-then-latent anger about priests and the church. Some of that latter stuff seems connected to the tombstone but also to something about her great-grandfather's second marriage as well as the annulment procedure for her sister's second marriage.

"Let me go these one at a time. Even so, I may not be able to make the intricate way they all weave together completely clear."

Father John cut in again. "I may be able to save you some trouble, Herman. I'm willing to guess that the issue with the tombstone concerns her great grandfather's having been denied the right to put a cross on top of it."

"Yes, but how did you know that?"

"That too is a long story, but perhaps this shorthand version may work. At the time of Danuta's death, the city wouldn't allow grave markers to exceed a certain height, which her relative appears not to have known when he purchased and erected his posh grave marker. When he found out, he was upset. I learned from talking with her that the matter had been one of those family stories told over and over. It was, therefore, as much an issue for later generations as it was for the old man. By now, I'm guessing, it has festered within your wife only to pop out as one of perhaps several unresolved matters she's finally chosen to show deep anger about ... or is *able* to show anger about."

"I think you've hit it, Father. But that's only one part of this weird and complicated mess. It seems that when her great-grandfather wanted to remarry, some priest — that's the way she and her family tell it — some priest said it was unseemly to do so within a year after his wife's death. So her great grandfather got married anyway, by a justice of the peace. And he only came back to the church on his deathbed.

"Apparently the family has always harbored that as evidence of the church's insensitivity and narrowness. So, not only did the church deny the man a cross for his wife's grave but also wouldn't marry him when he most needed a wife and a mother for his children. It's a wonder that Dannie and most everyone else in her family continued to go to church."

"I think I understand how it played out in her head, Herman. But just to set the record straight, the cross issue had nothing to do with the local pastor here or the church in general. It was a city ruling, stupid as it was, not a religious one.

"And as to the pastor in … Chicago, I'm guessing … I'm sure he was parroting the commonly held ideas of the time, but I can assure you that had her relative pursued the matter instead of walking away in anger or pride or whatever it was, he could have easily been married in the church. How unfortunate on both scores!"

"Yes. But those two things were *still* only part of a witches' brew within her. To add to it all, she had forever, I suppose — reluctantly — bought into the basis for those old Polish jokes. You know, how dumb Poles are. I was always able to laugh about that sort of thing, but she wasn't. I didn't know 'til just these past weeks how seriously she took that sort of thing. She's a bright and charming person, Father. It's partly why I married her. But apparently she always felt the needed to prove herself. I was more than a little blind, perhaps, but I never picked up on that. I guess when you're in love you only see what you want to see. I didn't catch that, and it apparently has exacerbated the rest of this negative jumble within her.

"Then, finally, there's the matter of her sister's annulment. I say finally because I assume this list of things is all there is to the equation. God help us if there's more!

"Anyway, a couple of years back her sister divorced a guy she had married in the church — divorced him because he was selfish, a drinker and abusive — and wanted to remarry. Jim Starret, the man she's married to now, is a wonderful man, and they are a deservedly happy couple. But when she went to the priest to arrange that second marriage, he told her there'd have to be an annulment first.

"I understand that's the church's normal practice, but I'm pretty sure she just took it as one more slap in the face from the Catholic Church ... on top of those others that her great grandfather had to endure and about which the whole family has been forever upset.

"She was told, as is not so unusual I'm led to believe, that she'd have to wait some months, maybe even a year or more, for that process to play out. Well, she got Jim in tow and went off to a J P to get hitched, and to this day they haven't gotten that straightened up in the church. And my Dannie got into a tizzy over that too.

"I guess you were the final straw that broke the camel's back, Father. What did you two talk about, you and my wife?"

"About that tombstone, and nothing more, Mr. Dudenbostel."

"*Herman's* fine, Father. I'd prefer that. But it was just that, you say? The tombstone?"

"Yes. Only that. And what I said shouldn't have upset her. I told her it was a silly demand from the city fathers at the time and it could now come to a happier ending. If she and her family wanted to add a cross to the monument, they could do so. I even told her about someone in that line of work who was honest, fair and would charge a reasonable cost. That was the entire extent of both conversations, Herman."

Herman sat silently, and Father John rose to bring in the coffee pot for refills. When he sat down again, he ventured tentatively: "That your wife couldn't really hear what I was saying, that she in effect insisted upon letting her anger rule her, tells me she's in need of psychological help, Herman. I'm even more convinced of that in the light of everything you've just told me. I hope that doesn't offend you."

"No, Father, it doesn't. I've come to that sad conclusion myself, although it has taken most of these past two weeks to do so. Part of me has wanted to deny it, as though it's somehow demeaning to accept and also as though I could maybe fix things by myself.

"I now realize I can't fix it and that she needs professional assistance. But I'm afraid about how to introduce that idea to her, and I don't know where to go for help. I'm especially afraid she may act out in the meantime … do something irretrievably stupid or damaging or even criminal. I'm in a hell of a deep hole here, Father. I don't really know what to do or where to begin."

After a few seconds, Father John rose and sat down on the sofa within reach of the other man, put his arm around his shoulders and said quietly: "I'm glad you came today, and I'm really glad I was available. We can get through this." With that, Herman burst into tears.

Father John rose and retrieved several tissues from nearby, gave them to Herman and waited for him to regain his composure, all the while praying fervently to the Holy Spirit: *Thank you for sending him here, but please don't stop pouring your mercy upon us both just yet.*

CHAPTER 38

When he was calm, Herman looked plaintively at the priest. "What do I do, Father?"

"Let's back up a bit, Herman. Your said you thought she was up to something for a while. Have you any idea what … or for how long?"

"Not really, but well before that prank in October, I'm pretty sure."

"I think I can probably help you with that," Father John said and moved back to his large chair. When he had settled in, he began by filling Herman in on the crossword puzzle innovation in the Post-Dispatch.

"Once that was announced by the puzzle editor of the Post, several such crosswords appeared in that paper. But then the St. Louis police reported a real crime based on that premise, a murder accompanied by a crossword puzzle. It was a big to-do, and I think the Post backed off from having any other such puzzles. It was shortly thereafter that *I* started receiving crossword clues in my Post-Dispatch paper box. That was early September. Actually, I was getting those clues before I found out about the Post-Dispatch connection, but as I traced it back, those notes didn't start until after those unique puzzles began in the paper."

"You think my Dannie was behind those things with you?"

"Well, just let me say that the October prank you spoke of was the leaving of one of those clues in my mailbox. I had informed the sheriff shortly after those clues began coming in September. At first it was an annoyance, but a curious one. Over time he and I began to wonder at the resemblance to that puzzle innovation in the Post, and we both started to suspect that maybe, just maybe, there was something serious going on with regard to me.

"Anyway, he checked out those tire tracks ... and the footprints ... in the snow. He could identify the tires as belonging to a Dodge van and the footprints at size eleven were probably that of a male, from the type of print and the impression. The person was heavier than a woman would ordinarily be and the type of print was from something like a work shoe. In retrospect he and I now figure that it was *very clever* ... " the priest slowly dragged out those two words " ... to deliberately leave prints in the snow that wouldn't be helpful. The van was, after all, from another state, and it was probably the only time a man, a male, left a clue behind my house.

"I guess you know that there are different tires on your brother-in-law's van from the ones he had in October." Herman shook his head to indicate that he didn't. "The recent check by the Sheriff's Department has shown that those on the van now don't match the ones from last fall. I'm not sure if that was deliberate or just a lucky occurrence ... and certainly a convenient one as well, at least for Dannie. Oh, and by the way, there have *never* been any fingerprints on those notes.

"In the light of everything we know now, how could it not have been Dannie who was responsible for all this?"

Herman looked shocked. "This is worse and worse." He seemed thoroughly devastated and after a short pause looked up in obvious pain. "Is she going to jail?"

"Goodness no. Not if I have anything to say about it. But, as I said, she needs help. And I'll do what I can to assist you in getting that for her." Herman's demeanor didn't change. "There's been no real crime, Herman," Father John added.

"Let me ask, though, have you any suspicion that she wants to act out, to do something to follow up on those clues?" When Herman didn't respond, Father John asked: "Bring harm to me?"

That got his attention. "God help us, I hope not." Now he looked genuinely alarmed. "But in her current state, who knows? I guess I'm afraid something bad could happen."

"I know you've said that her behavior recently has shown a side to your wife that you didn't know before, perhaps never even remotely suspected. So is it impossible to judge what she might be contemplating now? Or do you perhaps have an inkling as to how she might act at this point?" After a short pause, he said: "From all that you know about her, what's your best guess, Herman?"

He began crying again, but through his tears he managed to say: "I'm so befuddled right now that the best I can say is, *anything could happen.*"

The men now sat silently staring more into space than at each other. Then both started to speak at once, but Herman deferred to the priest, and Father John voiced what may well have been on the other man's mind: "I think we need to bring in the sheriff."

To forestall any further possible alarm from the layman in his living room, the priest said: "Mind you, I'm not calling Sheriff Toler so he can arrest your wife, but rather to be sure we react properly. It's in the best interest of everyone that we move before Dannie might ... I say *might* ... do something she'd regret. Is it all right to call Sheriff Toler, Herman?"

He nodded, and Father John reached over to the phone beside his chair. Several wordless minutes later, Larry Toler came to the front door of the rectory and was let in by a grateful Father John.

It took only a few minutes after he introduced the two men for him to brief the sheriff about their conversation. Then he put this to the lawman: "Am I right to assume we need to intervene before Dannie might act out?"

The sheriff nodded. "Yes, but it may be trickier than you think, Father."

That bothered not only Herman but the priest as well.

"What do you mean?

"She hasn't committed a crime. Any *intervention*, as you put it, has got to be well thought out and even better executed. Let's talk, the three of us."

Father John looked at Herman. "Are you okay with this, Herman? Are you up to it?"

He nodded. "I'll give it my best shot."

Father John turned expectantly to the sheriff. "So what are your thoughts about this, Larry?"

CHAPTER 39

"I want some way to peacefully approach your wife, Mr. Dudenbostel, to get her to voluntarily agree to a regimen of help. I have in mind some live-in facility, probably in St. Louis, where she can have ongoing therapy. But you're with the military, aren't you?"

"In a way, sheriff. I work at Scott Field. Of the civilian personnel there, I'm the number two guy. Why? Is that important?"

"I just thought you might prefer to go through the military for such therapy, for financial or other reasons. I wasn't sure."

"No, not necessarily. How expensive will this be, do you think?"

"I have no idea, but I doubt it'll be cheap. Are you sure it wouldn't be better for you financially to do this through the Air Force?"

"The bigger consideration for me at this point, frankly, is the quality of the help, not its cost. I can probably afford whatever that might turn out to be. But, since you bring it up, I can find out what's available within the service and where in the country that might take us to have it happen."

"Well, keep that all in mind then. But the core of the matter is that there should be ongoing help, and it will probably be a live-in arrangement. At least that's how this psychological layman sees it. Would you agree, Father?"

"I'm no more an expert on that than you are, Larry. But, yes, that makes the most sense to me. Yet I can't help worrying about how violent Dannie might turn out to be. Herman says he's hasn't any idea about that. All that any of us knows is that there's a violent undertone to those notes." The other two nodded.

"Oh! It just occurred to me. I should probably show Herman here what those clues spell out … and maybe the diagram that Paul did for us too. I think you already saw it … the latest one, especially, I mean. Right Sheriff?" He nodded.

"Let me get those for you, Herman." He was back in a moment and handed the diagram to him.

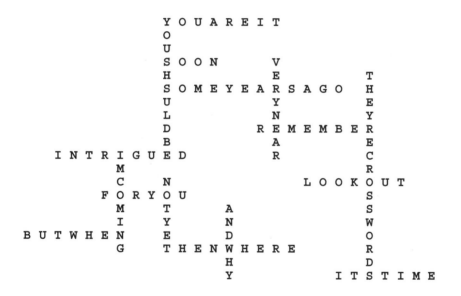

"What that spells out is: Intrigued / you should be / you are it / I'm coming / for you / but when / not yet / they're cross words / soon / then where / very near / and why / some years ago / remember ? / it's time / look out." He handed Herman those words that he had also copied.

"The middle part, *they're cross words*, was spoken to me on the phone after I had put an ad in the local paper, something that didn't pan out, but apparently alerted your wife. All the others appeared in my paper box, except for the last one, which came in the mail. And, by the way, that phone message had an altered voice that sounded male. It was like you might hear on TV or in the movies, the voice was lower and slower than normal. Does your wife have access to some kind of program that can do that, perhaps on her computer?"

"I have no idea. Not that I know of, anyway. But she spends a lot of time on the computer. She may have something like that."

"Well, in case any of that — the words and/or the diagram — means something to you, I thought you ought to have them."

Herman studied them for a moment and looked up at the other two. "They don't suggest anything. I still can't get over that Dannie would or could have done this."

"Please tell me," the sheriff said, "if they do come to mean anything to you. Who knows what might suddenly occur to you now that you have them."

"Where were we, Sheriff? Live-in therapy?" Father John tried to bring him back to the point.

"Yes. But approaching her is crucial. How to do that best, and where … and when … as well as under what circumstances too. Do you have an suggestions, Herman?"

"I don't know. Are you thinking I should do that? Or who, if not me?"

192

"Machts nichts aus to me. I mean, I'd be glad to do that, unless you think you or someone else would be better," Sheriff Toler said.

They looked at Father John.

"Oh, no! I'm pretty sure I'm not the one for that. I take myself out of the running, thank you both very much."

"I suppose so, now that I think more about it," the sheriff said. You don't seem to bring out the best in Mrs. Dudenbostel. So it's you or me, then," he said to Herman.

"Better you, sheriff. I'm a mess right now, and I don't think I'd be any better if I have to ask her to go into therapy, for God's sake. That'll just bring out that inferiority complex again, I'm afraid. No matter what or who, her initial reaction to therapy is *not* going to be positive, for sure. But ... " and he paused for what seemed a long time, " ... won't your talking about that also bring about negative reactions. I mean, all she'll probably see is jail in her future, if you're the one."

"I suppose there is that possibility. But do we have any other choices?"

"None seems obvious just yet, but we should keep talking. This is a huge step. I don't think we can be *too prepared* before we take it."

"Is there some way we could delay this, even just a little? Maybe there's something to ease her into this. I'm not sure what, but let's explore that possibility. Please ... !" Herman was literally begging the other two.

193

"You know that you — we — run the risk of something happening, the longer we wait, don't *you*?" The sheriff aimed that at both men.

"Yes, but depending on what Herman does to grease the skids, perhaps we could give it a *little* more time. What *might* you do in this regard, Herman? Can you just think out loud for a moment?"

"I could talk about those crossword thingies in the paper. Not sure how that would help, but that occurs to me. Or maybe I could take her on a surprise trip somewhere ... to get her mind off things. Or, I don't know ... maybe someone else in the family could talk to her."

"None of those strike me as helpful, Herman, I'm sorry to say. What about you, Sheriff?"

"I agree. Keep trying, Herman. Anything else come to you?"

"What if I talk about that tombstone? I could offer to pay for a cross for the top of it."

"*That might work,*" Father John said with emphasis. "But how do you get into that conversation with her?"

"Maybe that's where you come in, Father," Sheriff Toler said. "Hear me out. You've already talked with her about that ... twice. What if you tell her that you spoke with the monument guy in Cairo and ease into another discussion that way?"

"*Near* Cairo, Larry. Not *in* Cairo. But I *could* do that. Although, that could just as easily set her off."

"It's a chance we may have to take. But if it works, that could back her off from her anger and from whatever she *might* be thinking of doing because of it."

"Yes, but she'll still have problems that should be dealt with."

"Granted, Father. But this could buy us time, and we'd cross that therapy bridge when we come to it."

"So, what do I tell her? Shouldn't I maybe have some sort of carrot? A discount price … perhaps because the economy's so slow?"

"Think you can actually get a price break from your friend?"

"I can try."

"Let's say all that comes together. What do *you* think of that approach, Herman? Has it got a chance? And can you take the chance of waiting to see if it does?" The sheriff looked expectantly to Dannie's husband.

"I don't know. But why don't you first see about a price, Father? If that doesn't happen, I'm not sure there's any other good way for anyone to bring up the tombstone."

"Sounds reasonable. Let me go to the other room and make a call."

When he returned, he saw that the sheriff had refilled all the coffee mugs. "Good news. The economy *actually is* slow for him and he's willing to do me the favor of cutting a deal. And I didn't have to explain much about why I was asking. I just said someone here might need a cross put on top a tombstone, and I thought of him."

"Did you get an actual price?" Herman asked.

"No, but he assured me he'd do it for a cheaper rate. A lot depends on the style and size of what he's asked to do, and the kind of stone. He'll need to talk to Dannie first."

"Good. Can you live with that, Herman?" The sheriff looked expectantly in his direction.

He dragged out his response but answered affirmatively.

"So, when and under what circumstances do we do this? Timing's everything, as they say." The sheriff was unwilling to let the matter go on and on, running the risk of missing the right moment for such an important action.

"What's wrong with right now?" Father John asked.

"This very minute, Father?" Herman asked, clearly alarmed.

"No, not this morning. But just as soon as everyone agrees we could."

"I'll have to get back to work so they aren't able to tip Dannie off if she happens to call there." Herman seemed to be thinking more clearly.

"Of course. But then, when could I … should I … call her?"

"Why not tomorrow, Father? I'll go into work as usual tomorrow. And you could call me there afterward to let me know how it went. I don't want to come home to any further chaos. It would be nice if this works and I can come home and act happily surprised over her getting to do something that's really important to her."

"And if it doesn't work?" The sheriff leaned forward in his chair.

"Then you'll have to pay her a visit," Herman said resignedly.

"You got your mind right about what that will entail, Larry?" Father John had also leaned forward.

"I think so. But I'll first make sure all three of us are on the same page. Is that okay with you two?"

They nodded. And the sheriff rose to leave. "I'll let you two finish up whatever you had goin' on before I came, then."

It took only a few minutes for Father John to be sure he could let Herman go back to work. But he admonished him to stay in touch, just in case anything else developed or their closely hatched plan began to go awry. "And check that diagram and the words it depicts. Let me know if anything comes to you."

There was another prayer to the Holy Spirit as Father John moved his car back into the garage. And he did the best he could to prepare himself for the rest of the day and probable fitful night.

CHAPTER 40

He placed the call to Dannie at exactly ten o'clock the next morning. Her reaction to his carefully rehearsed bit of dialogue was calm and reasoned, neither hot nor cold. And he couldn't help but think of Revelation 3:16 about being neither hot nor cold but lukewarm and getting spit out. *Wow! How Freudian is that? But did I get her attention?*

"So, Dannie, should I have him call you? Or perhaps you may wish to give him a jingle. I can give you his number."

She paused long enough that he almost asked if she were still there. Eventually, she spoke … hesitantly. "I suppose he could call me. But not today. Tomorrow afternoon is much better. That way I can talk with my husband about it first."

"Glad to be of service. I'll call him right away with your message. His name is George, so you'll be able to recognize the call is legitimate when he phones tomorrow. Goodbye."

He got right on the horn to both the sheriff and to Herman. Only then did he call George and gave him a little heads-up about his prospective client, taking care not to mention how touchy that cross was for Dannie and some of her relatives.

To Herman and the sheriff he had said he wasn't sure if he got the brush-off or not, and he also wasn't sure what Herman would be coming home to that evening. But he cautioned him to act pleasantly surprised about the cross. And if he could read the tea leaves, he might volunteer to pay for it, perhaps as a birthday or anniversary gift.

"But most especially, Herman, you've got to let Sheriff Toler and me know tomorrow how well this went down. Don't miss that step, whatever you do. Okay? Call from work. That should be safe."

Herman agreed. And since he had talked to him before the sheriff, Father John and Larry were able to do their own reading of tea leaves. "What do you think, Larry? So far, so good?"

"I'm guessing so. But you talked to her. Anything in her voice that put you on edge?"

"She was hesitant, but otherwise I couldn't figure anything. I wish I could have seen her face, read her body language … that sort of stuff."

"We almost *have* to take it at face value. Right? I suppose we'll know better when Herman calls us tomorrow."

"Oh, oh! What if she doesn't bring it up?"

"Let's hope that's not the case. But if so, that's a definite red flag."

"And then what do we do?"

"I'll have a better idea about that once Herman weighs in. In that case, I may have to intervene. Let's hope it goes better than that. Isn't that your cue, by the way? Start praying, Father!"

"You mean *keep praying*, Larry. I've done little else lately. Whoever gets Herman's call can say he needn't call the other of us. Whichever of us gets his call can tell the other one. However, if either of us finds the slightest problem with Herman's report, you and I should get together at the jail and call him back. With me on one of your extensions, the three of us can talk together. Good grief, this is getting complicated!"

"You betchum, Red Ryder. Talk to you tomorrow."

Another long day was looming, as was a restless night.

CHAPTER 41

A recurring story in the back of his mind about a rabid dog had been bugging him for some days. A neighbor shoots a dog he thinks is rabid. The owner is upset and takes the dead animal to the vet, who examines him and says he wasn't rabid after all. Now the owner's mad at the shooter, who won't believe the vet because he thinks he's in cahoots with the dog's owner. The upshot is a feud, and three generations later it's still smoldering among the descendants of those two men.

Father John felt that wasn't just a piece of southern Illinois folklore. There was something quintessentially human about that tale, and it perfectly fit the Polovitski clan. He also couldn't help but think that his own life would be far less complicated if that family had gotten past their resentment about that cross and tombstone.

But life isn't lived in the subjunctive. What if doesn't cut it. Just deal with reality and get on with things, John. Otherwise you won't be any better than the guys in your story ... or the Polovitskis, for that matter!

So it was that he spent much of the next morning drifting between such musings and a perfunctory dibble-dabble around his desk trying to feel busy. Then the call came from Herman. "So how'd things go last night?"

"Strange! She didn't talk about the tombstone at all."

Father John was stunned. "But I called her as planned, Herman. And she said she'd take a call from the tombstone guy but wanted that to happen after she had a chance to talk to you about it.

He's going to call her today. But she didn't say a word to you last night?"

"Right. Nothing!"

"Tell you what, Herman. I'll talk with the sheriff and we'll get back to you. What number can I use? And when's a good time?"

At the jail the sheriff put his call through to the Scott Field number, and the three men were on the line with each other in jig time.

"Herman, we think this is certainly strange. I don't want to alarm you, but we can't figure what your wife is up to," the sheriff said. Father John sat silently in an office adjoining the sheriff's, nodding. He was able to see the lawman and was listening intently. "Father, have you any ideas about this?"

"Hello, Herman. I'm with the sheriff. No, I haven't clue one as to what this means. But the best I can figure is that we need to let it play out. I know that my friend, the monument dealer, will call your wife today. I'll give him some time to do that, and then I'll check to see how it went. Let's hope your wife has something to report to you when you get home *this* evening, and that she's happy about what she has to say, too."

"So, Herman, it's the same scenario for you, then. Look and sound surprised when she mentions the tombstone. At least let's hope that's what she'll do tonight. Whether she has tombstone talk for you or not, please get back to one of us tomorrow from work, just like today. Okay?"

"Okay, I'll do that, Sheriff. But last night didn't go the way we hoped, and that's not good. Correct?"

"Yes, it's not quite what we hoped for. Let's keep our fingers crossed about tonight, though," the sheriff said. "Talk to you tomorrow, Herman. Keep your chin up, buddy."

When they had hung up, Father John went over to Larry Toler's office and sat down dejectedly alongside his desk. "What's she up to?"

"The short answer is *no good*," the sheriff said. "But let's hope this is only a glitch, a temporary weird development that only her interior logic can explain … and that she reacts positively to your friend's call. Tell me what he has to say when you find out."

The priest deliberately waited for early afternoon to call George. "Did you make a sale, my friend?" he asked as upbeat as he could.

"Not yet, but she's interested. She'll run the figure for a nearly four-foot limestone cross past her husband. That all-inclusive, by the way. Installation's included in my estimate. And I gave her a healthy discount. Thanks for throwing me the business."

"Hope you seal the deal. Let me know how it goes. I'm curious."

"Will do, Padre."

He and Larry were talking minutes later. "What's with this *talk to my husband* stuff? She's yanking our chains, wouldn't you agree, Larry?"

"Sure sounds like it. Herman can tell us tomorrow. Meantime, just in case, I'm going over contingency plans. If she doesn't go for this, we may have some serious actions to take, and we probably shouldn't dawdle taking them, Father. I'll wait to talk to you tomorrow. However, I'm putting an unmarked car into her neighborhood ... just in case. Later!" He didn't mention it, but he was also stepping up his surveillance on Saint Helena's and its pastor.

Father John went over to church and spent the better part of an hour pacing up and down the main aisle trying to pray. He didn't have a good feeling about this all, try as he might to leave it to the Holy Spirit.

CHAPTER 42

Herman's call the next day was not reassuring. "Still nothing about the cemetery, Father. I'm worried."

"Don't mean to be brief, Herman, but I'm going to huddle with the sheriff. It may be an hour or more before we get back to you. But we *will* be calling. Hang tough."

"Now what? She's definitely playing us, and I don't like it, Larry. Got any tricks up your sleeve?" It had taken the priest only a few minutes to get to the jail.

"None you're going to like, I'm afraid. But any reason you shouldn't be checking back with your monument friend?"

"No, there isn't. It's something I'm planning to do. But I thought I'd talk with you first. Want me to call him from here?"

"Go for it."

The call produced more maddening evidence. George told the priest that the lady said her husband wanted to think more about it. It was an outlay that was *significant*, as he said she had put it.

"Did she say when she might get back to you, George?"

"No, she didn't. But I pushed her. I said I needed to know within two days because I didn't think I could hold that special price much longer."

"How'd she react to that?"

"Pretty cool. She said she'd try to persuade him because she'd like to do something about the cemetery stone."

"She actually said that? In those very words?"

"Yeah. Why? Don't you think she's really serious?"

"Well, how could I be *totally sure*, George?" Father John fudged. "But I really thought she would be, *hoped* she would be, anyway. Stay in touch, please, George. As I said before, I'm curious. And I don't want to be embarrassed by misleading you in this money matter. Your time's worth something, after all."

"Will do, Father. Sure hope she comes around. I'd like her business."

As Father John hung up, he looked at the sheriff. "She's playing a game. Why's she dragging this out, do you think?"

"My gut reaction is that she's planning something. I don't think she knows we're aware of what she's telling the monument guy. But if I'm right, whatever she has in the back of her mind, it can't be good. Problem is, she hasn't done anything yet for which I can get a warrant. But I'd bet my badge that she's *about to*. And if I'm right, I'd say it's you that she has in her crosshairs, Father."

"I wish I could fault your guesswork, Larry. But I don't see anything else that makes more sense."

"And ... "

"And I'm worried, okay? Feel better now that I've said that?" He had a lame grin on his face, something strangely between sheepish and bravely resigned. "But now what? How do I brace myself against something this tenuous?"

"Whatever you do, don't get creative with your schedule. Stay close to your routines. You have a better chance of watching your back that way. And so do I."

"So do *you*?"

"Yes. I've been all over you for a few weeks now. Tell me you haven't noticed."

"No, I haven't. Been too preoccupied. Just how short a leash have you had me on, Larry?"

"Inches, rather than feet. I mean, I've been watching your house with my guys. Thank goodness you haven't been out and about much lately. And I didn't want to tell you before, but you need to know it now. It's not Secret Service smothering, but close enough. Not bad for little-town America, if I do say so myself. And that's gonna continue, no matter what your reaction to it is."

"Ordinarily I'd be squawking, but under the circumstances, *thank you*."

"You're welcome. Glad you're not giving me any static. I'd have my way no matter what, you better believe. But this is easier."

"Okay, but still … what now?"

"It's her move, I'm sorry to say. We've got to sit tight and continue to try to stay informed. It's the only way we *might* be able to be a step or two ahead of her."

"We've got to call Herman. Given our suspicions, what do we tell him … or more accurately, how do we put it to him?"

"For one thing, I'm pretty convinced he's not in danger. That may be small consolation to him, however, though I'm not sure he'll be convinced we're right about that. But as to the exact words we use, that's trickier. We can't afford to spook him by being too cute and cagey, but I'm not sure how blunt we can be, either. Let's make sure,

Father, that we like what we come up with before you call his office at Scott Field."

It took almost fifteen minutes of word-crafting before both were satisfied. And they weren't sure after Father John's discussion with Herman that the man was as comfortable as they'd like him to be. They could ill afford his being nervous enough to alert his wife about their suspicions just by how he was acting, but they had to trust that he would pull off the delicate and dangerous game they felt he was being forced to play with her.

Herman promised to let them know anything that might come up in conversation at home regarding the tombstone. But he also would work on an idea the Algoma priest-sheriff combo had come up with. They wanted to know if could he possibly take a trip somewhere through the Air Force, some TDY equivalent to somewhere. The benefits of that would be, for him, his safety and for law enforcement, one less complication in an increasingly complex waiting game.

He'd look into it and get back to them.

Now, more waiting. And for Father John, house arrest, or the nearest thing to it.

CHAPTER 43

One drawback the duo noted was that they couldn't get a good reading on Dannie's body language and personal demeanor. And if Herman was actually going to get away, they couldn't even get at that information secondhand.

"I'd feel better if you or I could see her face once in a while, monitor her voice tones and inflections every so often, Father. We've been able to get the next best thing through Herman. If he gets away on a trip, we'll lose that. In effect, we'll be trading his safety for some intel that seems pretty important right now. But this whole thing may be getting close to a conclusion, anyway. Perhaps it won't matter in the long run.

"A bigger problem may be that he won't want to leave her *or* can't find a way to make that happen. It's obvious he's very much in love, no matter how weird he's found her behavior of late. I'm glad he's putting up with the idea of residential therapy.

"Of course, *that* has the promise of a happy ending. If he goes away, even just briefly, he might be worried that anything could happen with or to her, and that in turn could give him second thoughts. We'd better ride close herd on that if he swings some official Air Force jaunt to points unknown."

All Father John could do was nod in agreement.

Waiting was something the priest found far harder than the lawman did, and it was worse and worse with each day. Or so it seemed to him. Larry wasn't fretting much waiting around for Dannie to make a move. But it was certainly putting *him* on edge. Of course,

209

to the best of their common guesswork, he was the one being targeted, not the sheriff. He found himself taking the sheriff's concerns and precautions more seriously every day.

Herman had nothing new to report. Dannie hadn't broached the subject of the grave marker or any conversation with the monument dealer. It was clearer and clearer that she had an agenda and was more or less cleverly molding her words for everyone to suit that purpose. And when Herman told her he had to fly out to check on two other Air Force bases to check their compliance with something or other, she didn't seem phased by it. "I may have to also go to a third base, Dannie, depending on what I find out at the first two."

"How long will you be gone, dear?" she had asked almost nonchalantly.

"Two working days, maybe as many as four … probably not the whole workweek. I leave early on Monday."

"Stay in touch, dear. You know I'll miss you." She was all sweetness and light.

Such was the verbatim report the two got from Herman.

"You okay with this, Herman?"

"I think so. The trip has actually been pending. I just thought it would be later in the year. I convinced my boss that it would be as good if not better that it get done now, so he signed off on it.

"As to Dannie, I'm feeling such strain from what you suspect is going on with her, that this is something of a welcome break. But I still worry about what may happen to her, what she may get herself into, what she might do … without me there to keep her from something stupid or dangerous."

"I can only imagine," the sheriff said to him.

"Me too," Father John echoed. "I just hope you can trust the Lord to work things out for the best. The Lord and Sheriff Toler!"

That's where it stood until after the weekend. The law enforcement-clerical team agreed that nothing should be popping before then.

By that time an early Lent had begun. It seemed ironic to Father John that at a time when Christians focused on the passion and death of Jesus, he'd be focused on threats, cemeteries, crosses and God knows what kind of mayhem possibly erupting thanks to Dannie Dudenbostel. His own kind of passion. *How ironic!* He tried to steel himself as best he could.

CHAPTER 44

He didn't have long to wait. Even before the weekend, Mrs. D. called for him to meet her at the family monument so she could make some last-minute decisions about changes she was contemplating there. He took that to mean the addition of a cross, and said as much to her.

"Yes, Father. That's it. I just want to be sure I'm not running afoul of something else the city or church has legislated." There was a slight edge to her voice. "I promised to get back to the stone man as soon as I could be sure about those things."

Father John knew from a recent conversation with George that he hadn't heard anything from Mrs. Dudenbostel, let alone what she just said to Father John. Nonetheless, he agreed to meet her Monday morning at the monument, weather permitting. Neither Father John nor Dannie wanted to get wet or snowed on, so in the event of bad weather predictions, they were to reschedule.

"My guess is, I'm safe until then, Larry. Would you agree?"

"Sounds like it to me."

"But what about Monday? Do I just take my chances out there or what?"

"Oh, no. We can do far better than that. There's a clump of trees about fifty yards away from that grave on a little rise. I've done my homework, Father. The road that goes past the Dudenbostel plot runs just behind those trees. I can have a car there with several deputies in it. It'll be well-hidden. And they can be at the grave in a matter of seconds.

"But there's also a private mausoleum even closer than that. It's on the city side of the line, and I'm pretty sure I can get the key from the caretaker. One or two of us can be hiding inside there, with a full view of you and Mrs. D. I can also have patrol cars scattered here and there a little farther away for backup. All that isn't chopped liver, Father! Besides, I'm gonna put a wire on you. We'll all be able to monitor what the two of you are saying. With sight, sound and proximity, you should be safe. As safe as I know how to make you."

"Thanks. But it's not quite like having a Secret Service guy behind me who's willing to take a bullet. I mean, I'm still kind of at her mercy, right? You can't get there instantly, no matter how well you plan things."

"But there's more, like the TV pitchman says. It's still pretty nippy out, so you'll be wearing an overcoat, something thick. Underneath that I'll have you in a flak vest ... *very* bulletproof." He drew out the word slowly and deliberately. "You'll be safe from bullets, even stab wounds. Unless she has some heavy artillery hidden in an arroyo nearby or something like that, you should be okay ... no matter what she tries. One word of caution though. Protect your head at all times. And don't turn your back on her. Don't lose sight of her hands. Can't stress those things enough."

Father John felt far from 100% reassured by that last admonition but didn't say that to his friend.

213

Come Monday morning, well in advance of his appointment, he got outfitted appropriately at the jail under the supervision of the sheriff and then made his way out to the gravesite at the appropriate time. Her car was there already, and he pulled up in front of it, as instructed. She was to be denied any quick motorized getaway.

As he emerged from his car, she shouted at him above the noise of a small wind. "Nice of you to come, Father ... and so prompt too. Right at the stroke of ten, I see." She sounded all bouncy and frilly, the soul of joie de vivre. Her broad smile completed the picture of nonchalance and welcome.

That wasn't about to fool the priest or cause him to drop his guard. He knew that the county lawmen had been in place around the cemetery for some time, and he felt as safe as possible, given the circumstances. But he was still the soul of disguised caution.

He noticed that she was also in a heavy coat, and she had an oversize purse, something akin to a carryall: an odd accessory, but who knew about women's tastes and fashions? Perhaps it wasn't out of the ordinary. He nonetheless viewed it with a jaundiced eye and said as much quietly for the benefit of the police listening in. He was careful to bend down as he closed the car door while saying that, so Dannie couldn't see his lips moving.

As he got beside her, he asked: "What exactly are you concerned about, may I ask?"

"That's more my line than yours, Father. I want to be sure there isn't anything to get in the way of my putting a cross on top of this tombstone. It's going to be at least three feet in height, I'm led to believe. The stone fellow is going to eyeball it to get the proportions exactly right. Then he'll come back up here to erect it when I give him the high sign."

"Pardon me, Mrs. Dudenbostel ..."

"Now there you go getting formal again. Dannie, please!" She sounded appropriately clucky like a mother hen.

"Yes. Dannie. Well, pardon me, but we could have settled that on the phone. There'd have been no need for us to get out in this chilly weather. But now that we have, let me reassure you. There are no restrictions from anyone. You're free to alter the gravestone any way you wish."

"You don't know how relieved I am to hear that, Father. But just to be sure. I can have the stone person come here whenever it's convenient for him to do the work? There's nothing like some celebration planned that I have to avoid?"

"That's correct."

"And if there's a funeral on the day he comes ... ?"

"He's a professional, Dannie. He does this sort of thing all the time. He'll work it out."

"Oh good, then. My siblings are going to be so happy to hear we can finally do something about poor great-grandfather's wishes." She smiled sweetly at him.

But then she turned away from him and affected a sneeze. When she turned back she lost her handkerchief, and it dropped a few feet away from them both, because of the steady breeze. Her other hand was in her purse, although Father John only caught sight of that with his peripheral vision and didn't register anything unusual until later in hindsight.

He instinctively bent over to retrieve the handkerchief, and as he stood back up he saw that she had a fair-sized rock in her hand, probably dug out of that purse when she had her back to him. And she was in the process of bringing the rock down onto his head.

His arm flew up to block the blow, and the rock came down hard and painfully onto this shoulder instead. He kept his balance and was able to back away from her, keeping his distance even as she pursued him.

The sheriff and Hank Winstrom had already burst out of the mausoleum and were charging fast by that time. The patrol car had also kicked into high gear and was bearing down rapidly, its siren blazing.

Dannie stopped in her tracks, startled by the noise, and then made as if to retrieve something else from her purse.

Sheriff Toler's voice was loud above the wind: "Don't make any silly moves, Mrs. Dudenbostel. You'll be shot quicker than you can say *I'll be damned*." He was all over her by the time he finished speaking. Her arms were pinned to her sides by the sheriff, and Hank had handcuffs at the ready. She was completely subdued and in tears within seconds.

"You're going with us to my less-than-elegant country hotel, Mrs. Dudenbostel. Your Miranda rights will be read to you in the patrol car. You and I are going to have a long talk." Her total demeanor had changed. She now looked like a frightened little girl, and with good reason.

At the jail her bag yielded a small-caliber handgun that was registered in her name. Herman would later corroborate that he had made that happen when they were still living in the city. *For her protection*, he would explain. It was loaded, but the safety was still on. There was also a long-bladed kitchen knife in the bag. She had been loaded for bear, the sheriff would say later.

Father John had a nasty bruise on his shoulder from the rock, but the heavy coat had protected him from anything more catastrophic. Had he not succeeded in getting his arm up in time, however, it was touch and go as to whether he'd have a concussion, if not a skull fracture. He couldn't wait to rid himself of the body armor and heavy clothing back at the jail.

CHAPTER 45

"She'd thought this all out pretty cleverly, Father," the sheriff was saying. "The rock could have been left on the ground in such a way as to show that you tripped and fell on it. She planned to wear gloves, and actually had some on today, so no fingerprints anywhere. She figured the two of you would be alone out there, and I'm pretty sure she was convinced that was the case this morning. We hid pretty good," he said, smiling at the priest.

"But just in case, she also had a gun and a knife. She was prepared to use whatever it took. Although I haven't heard any from her — not yet, anyway — I'm betting she had stories ready for those scenarios."

"Did you get anything about why she had it in for *me* in particular?"

"I did. She was running at the mouth long before Hank and I finished with her — we had to spell each other, it was taking so long. I'd say the incident in the cemetery triggered a *really* manic episode. She wouldn't stop talking. If I didn't know better, I'd say she was proud of what she'd come up with and almost pulled off, and she wanted the whole world to know."

By this time, Father John had already left for home and come back again, returning once Sheriff Toler called to tell him he finally had time to talk. He had gone home almost immediately upon being rescued and spent the time putting ice on his shoulder and generally letting his adrenaline levels subside.

But now that he and the sheriff were back together, he wanted to hear the whole story, or whatever of it the sheriff had managed to extract from Dannie.

"She actually was bragging?"

"Seemed that way. She certainly wasn't shy with Hank or me. She went into the minutest details. Even more, she told us why she was so focused on you." Father John brightened up.

"You were for her some sort of Jungian archetype that represented the church and all its minions who had ever hurt members of her family." He paused for effect. "Bet you didn't think I knew about any of that stuff, did you?" He winked.

"And she was bound and determined to hurt you in several outrageously symbolic ways. She considered using a knife at first because the iconic you had stabbed her great-grandfather in the back by denying his right to embellish his wife's tomb. But she figured that was an unworkable weapon around which to construct an alibi. A gun was equally difficult alibi-wise.

"But having it appear that you fell, bonked your head on a rock and died from it … now there was a winner. No one would be around as a witness. There would be no fingerprints and, of course, the setting was a-number-one. And no one, so far as she knew, was aware that she was to meet you out there at the grave. She was determined that you buy the farm in front of some cross or other. Perhaps in church … but that had alibi problems too: it would be too hard to set that up in foolproof fashion. But the cemetery was perfect. And, of course, in her mind that's where it all started anyway.

"Meantime, she wanted you to suffer. That's why she dragged everything out so darned long with all those clues. And she was particularly proud of the Dodge van. She admitted that she just plain got lucky there, but she did seize the opportunity, and that gave her some *extra* pride. And when she learned that her brother-in-law had to change tires because of a recall, she got lucky again, she told us. I missed that recall information, by the way. Sorry!"

"Where did Herman fit into all this weirdness?"

"It's almost like he was a stage prop. She maneuvered him when she needed to."

"Have you gotten hold of him, by the way?"

"Yes. He's on his way back from out west. Should be in tonight."

"How's he taking it?"

"Not well, but trying for a stiff upper lip, or so it sounded like on the phone."

Father John nodded, as though that was no surprise. "So what do we do about the lady? Is she going to jail for attempted murder, assault or something like that?"

"Well, a lot depends on you, Father. We have a very extensive confession, very admissible in court, about the crime she committed and several others she was contemplating. But ... you could probably prevail with the court if you said you're willing to overlook her actions.

"Mind you, it's up to the DA to push for prosecution. But if you're okay with something else, and if the court hears that her lawyer will probably push for some directed verdict because of insanity — temporary or otherwise — it may want to save the time and expense of a messy trial and just have her put into therapy in some secure environment ... for as long as it takes. I assume you'd be okay with that?"

"You know I would, Sheriff."

"Good. Pat Kelly thought so too. He's prepared to speak to Judge Dixon on your behalf. He and I have every reason to believe that after they tap-dance around this a few days, that's exactly what they'll do. How's your shoulder?"

"You didn't miss a beat, there, Larry, with that question! Makes me believe you've orchestrated a whole lot of things already!"

The sheriff just smiled.

"It hurts a lot, but I saw Dr. Wilson before I got to the rectory. He assures me I'll live. I'm still trying to figure out how to get the most sympathy out of this. If it were my leg, I could limp, but I don't know how to convey the *enormous* extent of my injuries with just a bum shoulder."

He smiled and almost as quickly grimaced, as pain shot through his shoulder. He had already learned that exactly that sort of thing could happen sporadically and without warning. The sheriff chalked it up to bad acting, but the pain was genuine enough.

"I suppose it's out of the question that I talk to her."

"Right. Bad idea. Wouldn't advise it, and I'm pretty sure the prosecutor's office would outright nix it. Anyway, you'd almost certainly upset her, don't you think?"

"Suppose so. I just wanted to tell her I don't hold any grudges."

"Pretty sure she's in no shape to believe that. Best you wait. Save your energy for talking to Herman. Tell him. He's to get hold of me when he returns tonight. He'll either call from Scott or come here directly. I should know by then whether they'll even let *him* talk to his wife. Want me to alert you when he gets here?"

Father John said yes and went back to the rectory for some chicken soup and maybe even a small drink. He felt he'd earned it.

CHAPTER 46

He suddenly felt tired part way through that drink, barely finished it, turned the phone off and went to bed. He didn't even bother to tell the sheriff. *He'll figure it out.*

He almost didn't make it up in time for Mass and struggled through it. Over coffee afterward he realized he'd have to tell his parishioners. How to do that and how much to tell was beyond his capacity at the moment. *Maybe the sheriff can help with that.*

The sheriff! Good grief! I've got to find out about Herman from him. I wonder if the pain pills Dr. Wilson gave me will allow me to take a short nap before I see Herman?

He had to leave a message at the jail, but thirty minutes later Sheriff Toler called back. "I wasn't surprised when you didn't answer last night. And Herman wasn't put out. He had enough on his mind. I think he's taking the day off today. Want me to put you two together? He's going to get hold of me sometime this morning."

"Yes, definitely. But can you set that up for this afternoon? I'm going back to bed, but I should be available after lunch. And before I forget, I'm going to have to let my parishioners in on this. Would you think a bit about how much I can or should tell?"

After the sheriff said he would do both things — think about that and arrange for Herman to see him — Father John remembered one more thing. "Have you told the brain trust anything about this yet?"

"Nope. They aren't exactly on my list as need-to-know."

"But they're on *my* list for that, Larry. Would you call one of them and explain that once I get up from my nap I'll be calling them for a get-together? I want them in the loop."

"I understand and will be glad to get that message to one of them. Just understand that professionally it would be out of bounds for *me* to have done that."

"Gotcha. And thanks. Nighty-night!"

After lunch — longer afterward than he had planned — he awoke and called the jail once his head cleared. The sheriff had gotten hold of Jim Eisner, who would be alerting the others. "He said for you to take your time. They could get together with you tonight, unless that's too soon. You should call him about that. I also told Herman you'd like to talk. You want me in on that?"

"I hadn't thought along those lines, Larry. But now that you bring it up, that might not be a bad idea. Could that happen a little later this afternoon? Tomorrow's okay too. Whatever works."

"Sure 'nuff. I'll set it up and let you know. Here or your place?"

"I don't care. But my place might be homier."

"Done. You'll hear from me."

When all was said and done, Herman decided that the next day would be better, and the young guys were to come to the rectory that evening. Father John told Jim to bring some beer and snacks. "I'll pay you. We've got to celebrate, and I want to thank you guys. It won't be much, no elaborate gala or anything. But take care of the cost, please, Jim. I'll have money for you when you get here."

The evening was convivial and Father John was genuinely grateful. He promised not to show his scars and begged off any alcohol because of his meds: "Not that I really have any scars. But the shoulder definitely knows it's had an encounter it would rather forget about."

He edited the tale for length, and was gentler with the lady than a literalist interpretation would have called for. But he made sure they had the gist of the story and knew that he absolutely felt the young guys were a part of things turning out the way they did. "I'm glad to still be around, fellows, and you're partly *to blame* for that," he told them, smiling at his own whimsy.

They left early, in deference to their diagnosis about his needing some sleep. He took them up on the suggestion, turning in only minutes after they left.

He knew that the next morning he would need to promise the Mass crowd a fuller story for the weekend, the story almost certainly being all over town by now. He also made a mental note to clue the Beckers in on things as well … probably shortly after Mass. There would still be time for Herman and the sheriff after that.

He slept like a dreamless log all the night through.

CHAPTER 47

The Beckers gobbled up Father John's story like starving orphans, but he held them to secrecy so he could tell his own people on the weekend. He made them promise twice. "It's not that I don't trust you. It's just that I know how hard it is to put a lid on something this juicy." He asked them to pinky swear and let it go at that, although he got a kick out of how solemn they looked as they responded to his deliberately silly phrase.

A little after ten, the priest was in his living room with Herman and Larry Toler, who announced that nothing had been decided about his prisoner. He held out hope, however, that Dannie would be remanded for therapy. Herman said he was accepting that as the best-case scenario, although it was hard for the other two men to tell how resigned he actually was.

Coffee having been refused all round, the next to speak was Father John, who addressed his words to Herman. "I can only imagine that this ordeal has been just awful for you. How are you holding up?"

Herman delayed his response as though searching for words or trying to sort out his feelings, Father John continued: "I hope you don't think either of us has been manipulating you, Herman." He gestured toward the sheriff as he spoke.

That brought words to the man's lips. "Oh, not at all. I've seen for weeks how disturbed my wife has seemed. I'm grateful I could turn to you both. My hope now is that therapy won't take forever. I miss her already. I can't bear to think what it will be like if the treatment goes on and on. And anyway, who are you to be concerned about me? Look at what you went through, Father."

For the next half-hour Toler and Father John laid out the whole story detail by detail. They shared their guesswork with him, the attempts to get things right that sometimes were off the mark, and the risks they ran at the end when they brought things to a head, not only neutralizing his wife, but doing so with all the legalities in place.

"It was touch and go at times, Herman," the sheriff said. "Some of that you knew, some we kept from you. We were sometimes concerned about not wanting to overly upset you and sometimes about not wanting our efforts compromised because you might, however inadvertently, alert her about what we were up to."

"I understand," Herman said, although the sheriff wasn't sure how fully he did. But he kept that to himself and continued. "I hope you won't think that you'll be a pariah here in town once this all gets fully known."

"It is a concern of mine, frankly, Sheriff. But the Air Force may soon make that a moot point. A transfer seems to be in the works. This last trip of mine may lead to my being assigned to one of the bases I just visited. We've uncovered things that my boss thinks I'm the one to set right. Nothing's decided, but I could be gone in two weeks to a month, and I don't know if that's to be permanent or temporary."

"How will that affect you with regard to your wife, then?" Father John looked very concerned.

"That's one factor my boss is taking into consideration … first things first, though. We've got to find out about Dannie; then we deal with my job status."

"Is that stressful for you?"

"Strangely enough, no. Or perhaps I should say not yet. My biggest concern is Dannie. Other things, including my job, are quite secondary.

"But there is one other thing. I'm going to put that cross onto the gravestone. How can I contact the fellow who does that sort of thing?"

"His name is George and I'll get you his phone number. Just give me a second." He was back in no time with a small piece of paper. "That's his office number. Call him any time during business hours."

"I looked at that diagram you showed me, Father, the one with all Dannie's threats on it, and it gave me a rough idea of what that cross should look like. The bottom right of that design shows a very slender and long cruciform shape. With that thin obelisk-like shape atop the tombstone, I figure any cross that goes up there should probably be long and slender too. Not exactly like that design, but sort of like it. I'm no artist, but that's what I'm going to talk to this George about.

"I'd like to surprise Dannie so whenever she gets out of the program, or perhaps sooner if she's allowed to leave for part of a day, I can show it to her. I know it'll mean a lot to her … and to her family too."

Father John was touched and said as much. Herman didn't know how to respond to that. He just smiled shyly.

The trio broke up before noon, leaving Father John to some prayerful musings that he moved over to church to engage in.

He was surprised to realize that though his life could have been in danger, and actually was at the very end of things, he hadn't dwelt on that very much and was generally not that frightened … most of the time, anyway. He didn't attribute that to bravado, but more like to good fortune or *dumb luck*, as he put it silently to himself. But the more he thought — prayed — about it, the more he decided it was Divine Providence.

Once again, Divine Providence! Should I presume, Lord, that you have more for me to do, protecting me this way? Unless or until you show me otherwise, pardon me, but that's the way I'll take it.

CHAPTER 48

Time would prove to be kind to Herman and Dannie. While her therapy lasted over six months, much of that time found Herman away from Scott and heavily occupied with setting things straight at McChord Air Base near Olympia, Washington. The base had recently been joined to the nearby Fort Lewis for administrative reasons, and the newly named complex was known as Joint Base Lewis McChord.

He got back every so often to St. Louis to see his wife who was in a minimum-security civilian facility. He was able to take her out on a day pass after several months, and he truly surprised her on one of those trips by showing her the newly finished tombstone in Saint Helena's Cemetery. Afterward he would say he thought it helped to heal her.

By the time her therapy had ended, the two had agreed to sell their Algoma home and move to Washington. Herman had been assured that when his temporary assignment was finished, there would be a full-time job for him at McChord, so they made plans to move to nearby Dupont. He found that he liked the climate in the Northwest and was sure Dannie would too.

Father John recommended that they check out Saint Martin's Abbey in Lacey, just south of JBLM, as the signs now called the two military facilities: Joint Base Lewis McChord. "I'm sure you'll find the monks friendly and I think you may also like their liturgies. If so, please remember to support the parish at which you register, though." He had said that to Herman with a large smile on his face as he spoke.

"And say hello to the abbot there for me. We got to be good friends a summer ago when I was out there on retreat."

The Dudenbostels were gone to the West Coast before the next Thanksgiving. Father John wondered if any of their family would ever visit Danuta's grave again. But he was glad that Herman finally got the cross atop the gravestone ... glad for Danuta and her family, and glad for himself and his Germanic sense of closure for loose ends.

For Father John, the ordeal that had begun just after the dog days of August the previous year had ended in a chilly Lent with the promise of the joy and grace of an Easter Resurrection. And he warmed to that with gratitude as it unfolded with the weather losing its chill and the flowers coming up and the world spinning into the future.

He doubted that he'd stay in touch with the Dudenbostels now that they had moved away, or they with him. But he surely wouldn't forget them. Not the scare that Dannie put into him nor the sweetness and loyalty of her husband, Herman.

How strange ministry can be sometimes!

He never doubted the arrival of God's grace, but he was again reminded that he was no good at predicting its trajectory.

God must surely have a sense of humor.

To order copies of *CROSSWORDS*, please fill out the order form below, tear it out and enclose it + your check in an envelope addressed to:

PAX Publications   1405 Eastview CT NW   Olympia WA 98502
Please specify PRINT, or E-BOOK VERSION

Inquiries may be sent to the above address or to: jackfrerk@aol.com

---

ORDER FORM

Please ship _____ copies of **CROSSWORDS** by Jack Frerker

Retail price (**BOOK**): $20.00 (plus $4.00 per copy Shipping/Handling)

Retail price (**E-BOOK**): $10.00 (NO Shipping/Handling)

Phone: _____   E-mail: _____

Make checks payable to: PAX PUBLICATIONS

Payment of $_____ is enclosed

Signature _____

Shipping Information:

Name: _____

Address: _____

City: _____

State: _____   Zip: _____